MURDER BY HANGING

Beamish carried the table in from the studio, set it under the loft-trap, and from that combination was joyfully able to discover a small tear in the wallpaper at the right height and size to have been made by swinging heels. He raised his voice in excitement as he pointed this out to Mosley, but Mosley behaved for all the world as if other men's eagerness passed him by.

"Whoever did this came equipped with a complete hanging kit."

"Not at all a bad thing to do, if you ever go out on a hanging expedition," Mosley said.

Beamish came up from the carpet with a short length of cotton thread. "Do you know what this was used for?"

"You have an idea, Sergeant?"

"To tie a loop so that the noose was hanging at the right height to be slipped over the victim's neck. It would break immediately the rope took her weight."

"Finesse."

"So what sort of murderer is it who comes out tooled up strictly according to Home Office practice?"

"A man who enjoys his work," Mosley said. "There's one way in which he doesn't seem to have been equipped. There was no linen bag over her head. Do you know why that was, Sergeant Beamish?"

"Can't guess."

"He didn't want to miss the look on her face," Mosley said.

MISTS OVER MOSLEY

John Greenwood

BANTAM BOOKS
TORONTO • NEW YORK • LONDON • SYDNEY • AUCKLAND

All the characters and events portrayed in this story
are fictitious.

*This low-priced Bantam Book
has been completely reset in a type face
designed for easy reading, and was printed
from new plates. It contains the complete
text of the original hard-cover edition.*
NOT ONE WORD HAS BEEN OMITTED.

MISTS OVER MOSLEY

*A Bantam Book / published by arrangement with
Walker & Company*

PRINTING HISTORY

Walker edition published October 1986
Bantam edition / October 1987

ISBN 0-553-26897-X

Published simultaneously in the United States and Canada

*Bantam Books are published by Bantam Books, Inc. Its trademark,
consisting of the words "Bantam Books" and the portrayal of a rooster, is Registered in U.S. Patent and Trademark Office and in other
countries. Marca Registrada. Bantam Books, Inc., 666 Fifth Avenue,
New York, New York 10103.*

PRINTED IN THE UNITED STATES OF AMERICA

KR   0 9 8 7 6 5 4 3 2 1

MISTS OVER
MOSLEY

Chapter One

"Marldale?" the Assistant Chief Constable asked. "Whose pigeon?"

"Mosley's."

"Oh."

The Assistant Chief Constable bore the look that might cross the face of a woman who sees a cherished ear-ring swilled down the plug-hole of a bath.

"In that case, perhaps, you yourself—Tom—"

Detective-Superintendent Tom Grimshaw's stomach was beginning to behave as it had done on the only occasion when he had gone down a coal mine. He suspected that the ACC had recently enjoyed a round of golf. The ACC did not play frequently or well, but he invariably returned to the office refreshed and rededicated—and as often as not charged with some piece of delicately confidential information that was worrying him stiff. It seldom had any bearing on any case-work that Grimshaw had in hand. Most usually it had nothing to do with any crime of a nature that ought to be concerning a Criminal Investigation Department at all. And without fail it required something difficult, protracted and unpleasant to be done with elegant diplomacy at once. But a sortie into Mosley's jealously guarded territory behind Mosley's back was a refinement that the ACC had not brought from the clubhouse before. Grimshaw adjusted his mind to impending disaster.

"Witchcraft," the Assistant Chief Constable said.

"I beg your pardon?"

"A witches' coven in Marldale."

The ACC's eyes were becoming bulbous with the effort of willing the head of his CID to take him seriously.

1

"I don't know that there is anything still on the Statute Book—" Grimshaw began to say.

"Oh, please, Tom—don't think that this is *official*. This isn't a *complaint*—an early warning, rather."

The ACC spread his hands as if he were disowning the very thing that he was talking about.

"People get disturbed, you see. I dare say no law has been broken—but there are other sides to life, besides crime."

Grimshaw decided there was nothing for it but to listen solemnly for the next five minutes.

"When you say witchcraft, sir—you mean the evil eye? Black Mass—that sort of thing?"

"Oh, good God no, Tom. Nothing as sickening as that. Just hints of things that were not dreamed of in the philosophy of that fellow Horatio. A church clock, for example, that rewound itself after leaving the village ignorant of the time for three weeks."

"That must have wrought havoc with the pace of life in Marldale."

"A Rhode Island rooster who refuses to service his concubines."

"Maybe he just doesn't fancy them. I'm not sure whether it's possible for a cock to be a queer—"

The ACC displayed that expression of tolerance which allowed his subordinates their little joke: not more than one per session.

"And there is the very odd case indeed of a man who was able to predict to a nicety the score of each of his last three darts in an inter-pub league match."

"I should have thought that that was the object of the game, as played by most perfectionists."

"Ah, but this strains credulity."

The ACC brought out his pocket diary, on one of the back pages of which he had written down the details. He must be taking the matter very seriously indeed to have gone to the length of taking notes.

"Seventeen, treble nineteen and double six."

"That seems a rational goal for a man with eighty-six to get."

"Ah, but how was he able to announce in the bar of the Crook Inn a week previously that eighty-six was what he would need to get, and that that was the combination by which he would achieve it?"

"I don't know. How was he?"

"Priscilla Bladon told him."

"Priscilla Bladon?"

"Old maid of the said parish. Occasional poet, whose verses appear gratuitously from time to time in the pages of the *Marldale and Pringle Gazette*, who has for many years read the tea-leaves at the Marldale annual Church Fête, but whose previous life has otherwise been blameless. It is in Miss Bladon's house that the coven regularly meets."

The idleness—well, no, better call it the leisureli-ness—of life in villages like Marldale did, of course, give rise to gossip of a remarkably inventive character. But the ACC, having embarked upon his thesis, would resent in-terruption.

"It was Priscilla Bladon who predicted that the church clock would spontaneously wind itself and return to duty. It was Miss Bladon who forecast the impotence of Tommy Robinson's rooster. It was Miss Bladon who told Harry Akeroyd not only how many he would have to score at darts, but by what precise digits he was going to score it."

"I am sure that all these things admit of a rational explanation."

"And so am I, Tom. What sort of an idiot do you take me for? What I want you to do is find out what that rational explanation is. It might help you to know—"

The ACC picked up his diary again.

"—the names of Miss Bladon's associates. The coven meets regularly under her roof, and the two other partic-ipants are a Mrs. Susan Bexwell and a Ms. Deirdre Har-rison. Mrs. Bexwell is an ordinary housewife who has somehow fallen under Priscilla Bladon's spell—she is mar-ried to a research chemist in Flavour Controls, Ltd., down in Pringle. And Ms. Harrison is a social worker operating in Pringle—a professional young woman who certainly ought to know better."

Ought to know better than to be a social worker? Grimshaw wanted to ask. But he knew from experience that the ACC was unlikely to find that funny.

"You are suggesting that I should give this priority?"

Grimshaw asked. "The muggings in Bradburn are taking up a deal of time."

He knew what pressure certain district councillors were putting on to get that beastliness cleared up.

"The Bradburn muggings always happen at night, and you can pop up to Marldale in the daytime," the ACC said, as free as ever with other men's time. "This sort of nonsense disturbs a community, Tom—and I do not care for my communities to be disturbed."

His communities: he was becoming as patriarchal as Mosley.

"Sir. But do you not think that Mosley—?"

"I do not want you to put Mosley on to this. Mosley is too likely to make a heavy meal of it."

"What's the betting, sir, that Mosley knows all about it already? Very little goes on on Mosley's ground that he can't account for."

"I do not want Mosley to be involved, Tom."

"For my money, he'll already be involved."

"I mean involved by us."

The Assistant Chief Constable looked uncomfortable. He was a man who displayed his tensions and uncertainties in every tic.

"I was very fortunate to come by this information, Tom. I do not want my informant to be harassed in any way. The way Mosley would be likely to handle it—"

"I don't suppose, sir, that I might talk to your informant?"

Dangerous ground.

"I think on the whole better not, Tom."

He always resented the convention that allowed his officers to keep the names of their narks and grasses secret. He pounced on any opportunity to pay them back. Besides, he always got a kick from playing the detective: it happened rarely enough in his life.

"It will be much more interesting to see what conclusions you can reach starting from scratch."

Any assignment originating from this desk was guaranteed to be as difficult as pre-conditions and secret saving clauses could make it.

Chapter Two

Marldale has a triple connotation. There is the dale itself, a swooping declivity, generally mist-ridden and clad in forty greens of heather, bracken and tufty grass. It defies the elements in a tract that Boundary Commissions are forever shunting about between Lancashire and Yorkshire. Upper Marldale, not unreasonably, is a village at the head of the valley. When men in towns as ignorant as Bradburn and Pringle speak of Marldale, it is Upper Marldale that they mean. Lower Marldale lies at the bottom end of the decline, a distinctly lesser place, seldom spoken of even among the well-informed. Older men who did a spell of their wartime service in Lower Marldale usually prefer not to recall the fact: the hamlet was host to an army Glasshouse, *Prison* whose barbed-wired and Nissen-hutted compound is now decrepit and insanitary, and houses a commune of creative artists whose talents remain for the most part unacknowledged.

When Detective-Superintendent Grimshaw considered British winters, he often marvelled that any human tribe should have chosen to make its home on this offshore island. It could only have been some subtle act of race penance that had inspired a branch of it to settle under the dominating nebulosity of Marldale. And yet newcomers were still arriving—and remaining.

Why, in fact, did Upper and Lower Marldale exist at all? Grimshaw knew the answer—in theory: sheep. Sheep could maintain themselves on the flanks of the valley without the import of foodstuffs, and the men who managed and tended the sheep had to house themselves. Other men had come to quarry stone, then others to build more houses

5

and attend to defects in the health and plumbing of those living in them. Others came to trade in victuals and ale, in postage stamps and coal—and some to burgle, defraud and do violence to their neighbours. But crimes of more than ordinary ingenuity were relatively rare in the dale and were well within the professional capacity of Detective-Inspector Mosley, to whom the locality was assigned, together with a great many square miles of similarly occupied territory.

Mosley's patch gave little administrative anxiety to Detective-Superintendent Grimshaw, but this was not because he considered it safe in Mosley's hands. On the contrary, such petty wrinkles of unrest as Grimshaw did suffer on account of Mosley's area almost always derived from the fact that Mosley had been temporarily active in it.

When Grimshaw paid working visits to his subordinates' domains, he considered it a point of decency to let them know his intentions in advance. In this case he had omitted to do so, prompted not only by the Assistant Chief Constable's orders (which he was capable of ignoring) but by the intuitive, niggling certainty that if there was trouble on Mosley's patch, Mosley was likely to be found somewhere close to the nerve-centre of it.

Grimshaw was never entirely at his ease in country of the kind that he assigned to Mosley. He knew himself, objectively, to be a good policeman: clear-minded, sincere, informed-to-date and systematic—but he was half-consciously aware that he lacked something. Whenever trouble occurred, people in settlements like Upper Marldale swarmed from their cottages and crannies to tell Mosley all about it; they kept out of Grimshaw's way. When Mosley went into murky drinking-shops like the Crook Inn, Upper Marldale men became jovial at the sight of him; when Grimshaw entered, they quietly finished their drinks and slipped off home. There was something missing in his make-up. Was it the common touch? Or was it that he was secretly afraid of his intellectual, hierarchical and social inferiors? (Come to that, did Mosley consider himself superior to anyone at all—except possibly his Detective-Superintendent and the ACC?)

Grimshaw went to the Crook Inn. He had to—there

was nowhere else to go. And he knew nobody in the village, had no back-up informants to help assess the veracity of anyone who, in defiance of all natural laws, was prepared to linger and talk to him.

He was quite unexpectedly relieved to see that he had the bar almost to himself and even rose within grasp of joy to see the quality of the only other drinker. For he was a man in well-preserved early old age, with *retired officer* written all over him: in his moustache, in the hair cropped close at the sides of his largely bald head, in his ancient sports-coat with its cuff and elbow leathers and in his Western Desert corduroys. This was not the sort of man who would talk to him in some recondite dialect, then laugh at him for failing to understand it.

Major Hindle—as Grimshaw was later to identify him— nodded politely when Grimshaw came in. Clearly he regarded the pub as his regimental mess and himself under obligation as the senior officer present. Grimshaw ordered himself a half-pint of mild, then put into effect a set-the-ball-rolling drill of which he was rather proud—it showed, he considered, a creditable resourcefulness. He stepped out of the front door, looked up at the church tower and then came back in again.

"Is your church clock right?"

"Back it against any chronometer in the kingdom, sir."

"Glad to hear it."

"Mind you, thereby hangs a tale, as the kitchen-maid said to the gardener's boy. Rum bloody do altogether. Not that I believe all the claptrap that was talked at the time, you understand, but a man has to accept things when they happen. Still, you mustn't let me bore you."

"I assure you—I love local yarns—bit of a connoisseur of them, as a matter of fact. I say—what are you drinking?"

The Major patted an empty inside pocket.

"Bit of an embarrassment, actually. Left my wallet at home. Never come out with the price of more than one pint in my pocket before lunch. So I shan't be able to reciprocate. Unless of course—"

He looked hopefully at the man behind the bar.

"Unless Len here will allow me to sign a chit."

Len nodded agreement—not happily.

"Well, then—let me tell you this tale. And Len here will stop me if I utter a syllable that's not true."

Len pulled him a pint, which required no consultation.

"This all happened last March. Marldale church clock has always, it seemed, had a reputation for temperament. Vestry records are full of complaints, going back to the month that the thing was put in—and that was early eighteenth century. And so it went on, through the Napoleonic wars, the first war and the second. Until Peter Muller came to live here—oh, that's all of thirty years ago. German—ex-prisoner of war. They'd put him out to work as a farmhand, and he married a local girl, opted to stay on. But he'd served his time as a clock-maker in Stuttgart. And the work he did in this village on people's time-pieces was nobody's business. Nobody's business. Brought him in a small fortune. I'll swear every watch and mantel-clock in Marldale has been spot on to the second since the second world war. So one day the parochial church council had the notion of putting Peter Muller in charge of our church clock. They paid him an annual honorarium—fifteen quid—and for that he had to keep it oiled, wound, and going. Which he did. Until last March."

Major Hindle flushed his organs of speech with bitter beer.

"And last March the poor bugger had a stroke. They stuck him in hospital in Pringle. And the first thing we know here, he hasn't been away forty-eight hours, the church clock stops. I might say it caused great inconvenience."

He looked mischievously at Len.

"We didn't know when it was closing time."

"You never bloody do," Len said.

"And there was local controversy. There were voices in favour of putting the job out to tender, going as far afield as Bradcaster, maybe. Others said no, that would be unfair to Peter. Besides, word might get round to him, down in Pringle—and if he felt he'd been done out of the job that he loved, it might set him back no end. So finally we decided that we'd live without our clock until such time as Peter Muller comes home."

"If he ever bloody does," Len said.

"But that was reckoning without Priscilla Bladon."

"Gentleman doesn't know who Priscilla Bladon is."

"No, well—she's Priscilla Bladon. I'm sure the gentleman will take my word on that point. What matters is that she and a couple of others—their names wouldn't mean a thing to you—had been giving it out that they were going into witchcraft. Friday nights are special occasions, at Miss Bladon's place. Load of old cod's-wallop, that stands out a mile—but they did tell Tommy Robinson he was wasting his time putting that clutch of eggs under his broody. Didn't they, Len?"

"They bloody did."

"And then they told Harry Akeroyd arrow by arrow how he was going to win a darts-match for this pub. Isn't that true, Len?"

"It bloody is. Cup's up on yon bloody shelf."

"So when they let it be known that they were going to get the old clock going again, it wasn't easy to get odds-against that they'd fail. Though I must say, I'd started to say goodbye to my money, when I saw how long it was taking them. They did a moonlight dance in the churchyard, all around the graves. Had an old wind-up gramophone stood on top of the Mawdesley vault. Kept playing the same record over and over again."

"Horrible bloody thing."

"The *Danse Macabre*," Hindle said. "Saint-Saëns. Went on for hours. Must have played it thirty times. Then suddenly the old clock boomed out. One in the morning. Spot on the minute, too."

"Makes you bloody think, dunnit?"

"I'd have thought midnight would have been more appropriate," Grimshaw suggested.

"That's what we all said. Only Priscilla reminded us we were on British Summer Time. So," the Major said, ordering his round, which Len duly noted on a pad under the counter, "you may conclude that Upper Marldale is a rum community."

"But what lies behind this witchcraft?" Grimshaw asked him. "Presumably they are reasonable women."

"Admitting for the sake of argument that the breed exists, I'd say the simple answer is politics." And the Major screwed up his face in distaste.

"Nay," Len said. "It was all done to get at her in the Old Tollhouse."

"Politics," the Major repeated, with force but without rancour. "Red-raggers, all three of them. It was all done in the first place to divert attention from what was happening about Ned Suddaby's field. Mind you, I'm not saying *how* it was done. That's another question altogether."

"Yes, well, her in the Old Tollhouse had her own ideas about what should be done with Suddaby's. And they hate her guts."

"Who doesn't? But I still say you're wrong, Len. Mrs. Cater didn't join battle until later on. The council had already got the planning people in before she put in her bid."

"Aye. Because till then, nobody knew the field was coming on the market."

The Major turned apologetically to Grimshaw.

"You must excuse us if we seem to be talking in riddles, sir. Little things loom large in Marldale. Just passing through, are you?"

Grimshaw was ready for this.

"I've been seeing the name of the place on the signpost on the main road for donkeys' years. I've always meant to come up and take a look."

"Not much to see, I'm afraid. Church is mostly restored—and badly. Nearly as much new building in the village as there is old—though we ought not to complain: we don't want the place to die, do we? You're not from round these parts, then?"

But this was a subject from which Grimshaw wanted to escape as neatly as he could. These bar-room quizzes about a man's persona could be astute and wearing. He finished his drink, took his leave and walked out into the street, now sunlit. The grey mountain mists of morning had lifted while he had been in the pub.

It was true that there was a fair amount of new residential development in Upper Marldale—in-filling, mostly, and not insensitively managed: all in the local stone, with

due regard to contouring and roofing materials. There was
a certain affluence here. Many of the newer houses were
detached, and what must be wives' cars stood on their drives.
This led to interesting speculation: these people must be
either retired or commuters to towns that lay ten, twenty,
thirty miles away. They were people who could have chosen
other places to live—so why come to Marldale? The streets
of Marldale were sunlit, on the average, for not more than
a hundred days a year—and for only a minuscule part of
the day at that. Was it possible that these folk had caught
their first sight of the place on one of its minority days and
had been charmed by it? Marldale had a small sub-post-
office, a one-time general shop that had been taken over
by a chain, and was now trying to be a supermarket in an
area not more than twice that of a cottage living-room. It
had no doctor, no chemist, no fishmonger, no street lighting
and no sewerage. Its school had been closed four years ago,
its constable removed last year and the police-house sold.
There was a weekly shopping bus into Pringle, now under
threat. Mosley country, *par excellence*. Mosley detected
crime in dozens of villages like this. Or rather, in nine cases
out of ten, he deflected crime by anticipating it. Mosley
would know by name two thirds of the people in Upper
Marldale. How often, Grimshaw wondered, did he come
here? Mosley's working diary, which standing orders required him to submit, was a suspect document. Grimshaw
had long believed that it contained only those items that
Mosley cared to have known.

Grimshaw walked to the southern extremity of the village and there he came across a dwelling that did not seem
to belong to the rest of the community. It had started its
existence in the eighteenth century as an irregular polygon,
with quaint chimneys, lattices and mullions, conceited cren-
elations and amateurish pargeting. Then, in an all-permissive
pre-planning era, it had taken unto itself a brick annexe
overpoweringly bigger than itself. Its garden was exces-
sively overgrown, or at least its outer boundaries were. Its
privet hedge was so tall that it was difficult to see how,
short of scaffolding, a man could ever trim it back into
control. Its shrubs and bushes had been allowed to go their

own way so luxuriantly that very little light could penetrate
to the windows nearer the road. It must be impossible to
live in the rooms of the polygon without permanent artificial
light. Grimshaw could only hope for the occupant's sake
that the other side of the house was more accessible to
daylight. He crossed the road in the hope of seeing something of the interior of the house, but all its ground-floor
curtains were drawn to within their last two inches. He was
able to form no impression of what kind of home had been
so blatantly concealed from public curiosity.

The entrance to the property was through a gate outside which a small van was parked, a vehicle with rusted
wings and sills that looked unlikely to pass its next MoT
test. Grimshaw was within about five yards of this gate when
a woman's voice erupted within the grounds.

"When I commission a task, I expect nothing short of
consummate workmanship."

Her voice was a vibrant contralto, her diphthongs richly
rounded, her vowels those of the self-satisfied south of the
kingdom. Even if the message she was delivering had been
a pleasant one, her tone would be suspect in Marldale.

"I shall deduct fifty pence from the price we agreed."

A man with a ladder balanced over his shoulder and a
bucket in each hand came out of the gateway, his back
hunched in dudgeon: a window-cleaner. He was about to
clamp his ladder to the roof of his van when Grimshaw came
abreast of him.

"Sir!"

His eyes looked into Grimshaw's with a sort of canine
appeal.

"Could I ask you to come and look at something, sir?"

It was not a situation that appealed to Grimshaw, but
at the same time he saw the tactical opportunity. He went
in at the gate and was able to get a proper view of the house.
And it was indeed only on the side nearer the road that the
windows were obscured by a jungle of foliage. The other
three sides visible from the drive were mostly occupied by
a reasonably well-kept lawn, beyond which lay the patio
and French windows of the annexe.

On this patio a woman was standing—a woman in

her sixties, Grimshaw judged, height about five feet four,
powder-grey hair in a vintage Beatle-cut, wearing lavender-
coloured slacks that flattered neither her thighs nor the
contour of her stomach.

"Now I ask you, sir—can you see a smear on that
window?"

"From this distance, no—I have to admit that I can't."

Grimshaw utilized the next five seconds to see all he
could—he had the feeling that he was not going to be
encouraged to remain long on the premises. He moved his
position so that he could examine the glass from a different
slant. Through one of the French windows he saw an artist's
studio: an easel, trays of jars and brushes, a grubby sink
and a paint-spattered white overall thrown over the back
of a battered kitchen chair.

"And who, may I ask, are you?"

Her from the Old Tollhouse—whose guts everyone in
Marldale hated—including Major Hindle. Certainly no one
in this county was likely to love her for her initial impact.

Grimshaw could see nothing wrong with the window-
cleaning, but he was acutely aware of the wisdom of non-
belligerence.

"Is there some business you wish to see me about?"

"No, ma'am. I came in at the invitation of this gentleman."

"He has no right to invite you or anyone else to come
on to my property."

"I apologize, ma'am, and shall withdraw forthwith."

Lamentably lame, he knew—and yet it seemed ex-
traordinarily effective, for it left her without riposte. Grimshaw and the window-cleaner came out of the gate together.

"Brass-necked bitch!" the window-cleaner said.

"In these parts, she's going to run out of people willing
to work for her."

"She has already. She ought to move out to the bottom
of the valley. Then she could spend all her time with her
freaks."

Grimshaw did not know at that stage who the freaks
were, but he did not want to hang about asking questions
within possible hearing of the Tollhouse. He said goodbye

to the window-cleaner and walked back into the heart of
the village, strolling the length of one or two streets that
he had not yet visited. He found a tobacconist's and news-
paper-shop and one that hopefully offered treasures to tourists: lamb's-fleece rugs, high-priced hand-loom weaving,
cumbersome local pottery and cheap basketwork from the
Far East. There was also a branch of the County Library
(open two afternoons a week) and a Community Centre that
looked as if it had not been entered for months. And that
was Upper Marldale. Two women were gossiping outside
the supermarket. One man was wheeling a bicycle, across
the saddle of which he had roped a rabbit-hutch, and they
were the only inhabitants of Marldale who cared to be out
in the unaccustomed sunshine.

But then Grimshaw heard something that halted him
in his tracks. It was a man's voice, and it came from a
gateway which he could not at the moment properly see.
It was saying, "Well, goodbye, Miss Bladon. I've made a
note of the date and time of your next meeting, and I'll be
present if I possibly can. If I don't show up, I wish you well
in the new experiment."

Grimshaw knew that voice, and he knew the little man
who now came out on to the pavement, knew his black
homburg, his flapping raincoat and robust, dusty boots. It
was a combination that he sometimes dreamed about at
night. Mosley waved to him cheerfully.

Chapter Three

There had, of course, been previous occasions when Grimshaw had seen a smile on Mosley's face: usually when he had been proved right after a long battle of attrition over some pathetic triviality.

"I'd been expecting you to be along," Mosley said. "Have you had lunch yet? They do a good ploughman's at the Crook."

But Grimshaw was diffident about going back into the pub. To be seen in there talking shop with Mosley was sure to expose him as a policeman, and that seemed undesirable this morning.

"I'm a bit pressed for time, Mosley. I have private business in Pringle early this afternoon, and I'd like to get over there as soon as I can. I'll grab a snack there if *tempus* permits."

"In that case, you can give me a lift as far as Denniston."

Mosley was a past master of the art of getting other people to ferry him about. Grimshaw could hardly refuse. They climbed the hair-raising road back to the highway, several times within an inch of the sheer drop over the edge in order to give priority successively to a sheep, a down-coming milk-tanker and a Junior School on a field studies expedition.

"You say you've been expecting me?" Grimshaw asked.

"I gather that Mrs. Cater has been to see the Assistant Chief Constable."

"Mrs. Cater?"

"She lives in the Old Tollhouse," Mosley said.

So the ACC had not picked this one up on the links. Mrs. Cater must have asked to see the Chief Constable

15

himself, which was about the only way outsiders got into the office of one of his deputies. Grimshaw did not admit that he had entered the Tollhouse grounds. There were times when it was fitting for there to be a gap of mystery between senior officer and his work force.

"You know the lady, do you?"

"I have met her."

There was nothing in Mosley's tone to indicate the sweetness or otherwise of their relationship. Grimshaw could not rid himself of the feeling that in his taciturn way Mosley was mocking him to his own satisfaction. He concentrated on negotiating a hairpin bend, where the road sank into a hollow to cross a fussy little brook.

"Mosley—what is going on in Upper Marldale?"

"That is an interesting question," Mosley said.

"I have heard unhealthy rumours, Mosley."

"I haven't quite fathomed everything out yet."

"You haven't?"

That was a relief. How many times had Grimshaw known Mosley confess to ignorance of something that was happening in his realm? Ever?

"No. There are reports that do not admit of ready explanation."

"Such as?"

"Such as the sudden death of a man's four rows of winter cabbages."

"Weed-killer, Mosley?"

"Apparently not. I thought it worth getting Forensic to take a look at a soil sample. They found no trace of chemical interference."

Mosley had had recourse to scientific method? *Mosley* had been sufficiently worried to probe deeper than barroom talk and old women's stories?

"And the cats have been behaving in a most peculiar manner in Upper Marldale," Mosley said. "All the cats."

"The cats?"

"They have been refusing to be put out at night. Even the most adventurous of them, even the incorrigible nocturnal prowlers—they have either been remaining stubbornly in their homes, or else they have been found cowering in sheds or hiding under piles of rubbish."

"You believe all this, Mosley?"

"I spent half a morning last week, interviewing cat-owners and cross-checking."

It was not to be wondered that so many of his routine returns were outstanding.

"I am sure there is a perfectly natural explanation," Grimshaw said.

"One would think so. Yet it seems particularly odd that this peculiar feline behaviour should have been predicted."

"It was, was it? By whom?"

"By a Miss Priscilla Bladon, a retired school-mistress, now approaching her eighties. Well—she has never actually qualified as a teacher—but she was uncertificated head-mistress of the Upper Marldale Primary School for many years. I know that Miss Bladon lays claim to extraordinary powers. In fact I attended a so-called coven at her house only last week, and certainly there were phenomena that cannot be accounted for in everyday terms."

Grimshaw had to reverse twenty yards to give precedence to a Post Office van. When he spoke again it was in widely separated words and a quavering voice.

"You—attended—a—coven—Mosley?"

"I thought I had better," Mosley said, "since they throw open part of their proceedings to the public, and some of the more nervous souls in the village have been expressing concern."

"I see. So what is the *raison d'être* behind this coven, Mosley?"

"That is something that I still hope to discover. The general public are excluded from the business part of the meetings."

"And the woman at the Tollhouse? She is also connected with these self-styled witches?"

"Far from it. Some people believe that she is the reason why they have taken up witchcraft. They believe it is the only way to discourage some of her activities."

Chapter Four

It was on the Friday night after the coven's next meeting that Mrs. Beatrice Cater's activities were discouraged for all time. Ernie Hurst, the Upper Marldale milkman (who came from Pringle) entered the Old Tollhouse to find her hanging from a hook that had been driven into a beam in her living-room by, one assumes, one of the original Tollkeepers.

It was rather less than a minute after seven o'clock that Ernie Hurst made his discovery. The Tollhouse was his first call on entering the village, and local by-laws were unambiguous that no house-to-house deliveries were to be made in Marldale before the stroke of seven.

Asked, as he was several times within the next two hours by ascending ranks of investigators, if it was his normal practice to enter a woman's house, and indeed her living-room, in order to deposit her daily pint, her orange-juice and her cream, Ernie replied with steadily diminishing patience that it was Mrs. Cater's cat, Boudicca, who was at the bottom of this daily ritual.

"Rum bloody name for a cat, innit?" asked the resident constable from Pringle, who, fired by the mystique of sudden death, was on the scene from his home five miles away within three quarters of an hour.

"Well, she was that sort of woman, wasn't she? Anything she had she had to have a rum bloody name for. How the hell did she get herself up there, do you reckon, Sid?"

Beatrice Cater was hanging from the beam by about eighteen inches of rope. Given that the room was eight feet high, that the beam was six inches thick, that her height was five feet four, and that her neck had been elongated by about four inches in the course of her terminal experi-

18

ence, her toes were actually in contact with the ground. They could not, however, have gained enough purchase to give her useful support if she (or an assailant) had undergone a last-minute change of mind. It rather looked, even to one with the intellectual limitations of PC Bowman, as if an assailant must have been involved, because there was no sign that any chair or stool had been stood upon to enable her (or an outsider) to fix the rope to the beam. Nor was it apparent that she had kicked aside any article of furniture to accelerate her irreversible despatch. The constable also noticed that coffee and some sort of liqueur for four people had been served, and that the hostess had not considered it desirable—or had not had time—to wash up the cups and glasses before hanging herself (or being hanged).

In accordance with received practices, PC Bowman got Ernie Hurst to help him down with the body, in order to ascertain that death was as actual as appeared to be the case and to apply resuscitatory drills if applicable. That these would be superfluous was apparent from the manner in which Mrs. Cater's cervical vertebrae were incapable of holding up her head. Although he normally lived within a sort of emotional armour-casing in the face of death and calamity, PC Bowman was relatively distressed by Mrs. Cater's head and its grotesque independence of its accustomed anatomical support. For several days he introduced this topic into all his conversations with all men.

"I reckon she's a write-off, Sid."

"Oh, aye. Not much point in towing her to a garage. What were you saying about her cat, Ernie?"

"Boudicca?"

"I still think that's a rum bloody name for a cat."

" 'If ever you see her waiting to be let in, Mr. Hurst,' she told me, 'let her in.' And four mornings out of five she was waiting to be let in. Funny thing—"

The milkman furrowed his brow. Anything inexplicable was a rare event. He was a man who readily accepted the most immediate explanation for anything.

"Funny thing. I opened the door this morning, and she wouldn't go in. You know, I reckon animals sometimes know things, Sid."

"Happen."

Bowman wrapped Mrs. Cater's telephone in his hand-kerchief, as he had been taught by TV police procedurals, and rang through to the desk sergeant at Bradburn, who initiated action in several well-established directions. Thus Detective-Superintendent Grimshaw received the news while engaged upon the third and final phase of his breakfast.

"Suicide?" he asked, at the mention of hanging.

"The reporting constable seems to have his doubts, sir."

"Who's that?"

"Bowman, sir."

"Christ! Scene of Crime?"

"On their way."

"Coroner's sergeant informed?"

"I am the coroner's sergeant, sir."

"Inspector Mosley told?"

"Can't find him, sir."

Grimshaw thought fast. Just for a change, he was going to make this his own case. He could give Mosley something innocuous to do on the periphery, if that was ultimately unavoidable. Grimshaw went back to his toast and marmalade. There was no point in arriving there too soon, and simply getting in the way of the Scene of Crime team. He did a little more thinking about Mosley. Yesterday he had been convinced that he had been very astute about the Inspector; now a little shrug of doubt was beginning to take the edge off his third and last cup of tea.

He had known—because Mosley had told him—that last evening Mosley had been intending to sit in on a meeting with the Marldale witches. But he had prevented Mosley from attending. He had arranged for him to be otherwise occupied: organizing and assessing questionnaires about the Bradburn muggings, and personally supervising an on-the-ground check of nightbirds who claimed any pretext to be on the streets of Bradburn after dark. This, he told himself, was an essential task, in which it was even conceivable that Mosley might turn up something useful; though it was, his second-echelon brain-cells tried to remind him, doubtful practice to take an officer off an enquiry, even an unreported one, that his teeth were already well into. Still, the Assistant

Chief Constable's say-so had been unequivocal: he did not want Mosley involved.

So, really, it was an uncalled-for act of masochism to be tormenting himself with the incipient niggle that if Mosley had been in Upper Marldale on the previous evening, Mrs. Beatrice Cater might still be alive.

The Detective-Superintendent had one more thought before leaving home for Marldale. He rang his office and asked for Detective-Sergeant Beamish to be made available from D Divison. Grimshaw's sergeant-clerk smiled as she dialled the Chief-Inspector, D: so Tom was going lone patrol on this one—and making sure that it got solved.

Chapter Five

The Scene of Crime team were a group who knew each other's ways and were led by Inspector Heathcote, an aspiring type who lived in the undying hope of solving something big before the main body arrived. He had solved any number of little cases in time to save the investigating officer any work, but so far they had all been too unimportant for a commendation.

Heathcote and his satellites were hard at it when the main body, in the person of Grimshaw, pulled into the drive of the Old Tollhouse. Men were dusting for dabs, measuring the ten-inch depth of drop, photographing the carpet, taking coffee-dregs for analysis and labelling plastic bags that contained, among other things, a short length of rope, a bundle of bed-sheets and various wisps of hair.

"Her bed appears to have been slept in by two people," Inspector Heathcote said, "although I'm given to understand that the lady lived alone."

"Have you talked to anybody? How old was she?"

"Late sixties, that's local opinion."

"Some people are never past it, so I'm told," Grimshaw said, his own sex-life inevitably crossing his mind: unexciting, definitely not moribund, though somewhat depressingly predictable. "Don't forget dog-ends and so forth. Might come in for saliva tests."

"Already attended to, sir."

That was the trouble with all this ancillary teamwork that they had to go in for nowadays: it was all too easy for the mastermind to be made to feel superfluous. Grimshaw went outside to cast his eye over the surroundings. No pleasure would have come more welcome to him than the chance to call Inspector Heathcote and draw his attention to a print in a flowerbed or reversing tyre-marks in the gravel. But he found nothing—unless—

Grimshaw moved closer so as to be able to examine a window-pane from an angle that he had not been able to manage yesterday.

"Inspector Heathcote!"

"Sir!"

"Curious-looking smear on the window here. Take a swab of it, will you, and put it in with the rest of your samples."

"Will do, sir."

And at that moment a large and overfed tabby cat came out from behind a pile of yard-rubbish and rubbed herself against Grimshaw's ankle, her tail quivering vertical.

"Oh, how do you do?" Grimshaw greeted her, always at his best with strangers whom he could trust not to be rude to him. The cat miaowed piteously and changed ankle and angle.

"Oh dear. Hasn't anyone thought of giving you anything to eat? I suppose with all that's going on people have lost all sense of priority. Now I wonder if that milkman bothered to leave anything, things being as they are?"

It had been mentioned in the first telephone call that it was a milkman who had found the corpse. This was important: the person reporting the discovery of a body was, according to statistics, a very likely suspect.

"Inspector Heathcote!"

"Sir!"

"There's a cat here requiring to be fed. We must always behave sympathetically towards the bereaved—it's in standing orders."

"Sir, I've done my best. I can't get the animal to come in."

Grimshaw looked over his shoulder, and true enough the cat had stopped a couple of feet short of the threshold and was glowering in at the open door with her back arched, her upper lip curled back and the decision to spit quite obviously close to the surface of her mind. Grimshaw stepped forward with his hands on his knees, bringing himself down to sympathetic cat-level.

"Puss, puss!"

The creature put a brave paw forward, then suddenly snarled, spun about and shot streak-like behind the rubbish from which she had emerged.

"Makes you wonder if animals sometimes know things," Grimshaw said. "Inspector Heathcote—did that milkman leave anything?"

"Milk and cream on a corner of the kitchen-table, sir."

Grimshaw went and found a saucer in one of Mrs. Cater's cupboards, filled it with cream, carried it out and set it down by a corner of the junk-pile.

"Inspector, I'm going to make some enquiries in the village. When you've finished, or if you want me for anything, I'm sure you'll have no difficulty in locating me. My every movement will be a local event. And if Detective-Sergeant Beamish arrives, send him after me."

He drove slowly towards the Upper Marldale nerve-centre, but seeing a milkfloat parked fifty yards short of the High Street, pulled up and waited for Ernie Hurst to come out.

"Good morning. Am I to understand that you are the man who discovered the unhappy scene at the Old Tollhouse?"

"Correct, sir."

"Detective-Superintendent Grimshaw, Bradburn Headquarters. And you are?"

"Ernest Hurst, Pringle Model Dairies."

"Is it normal procedure for you to enter premises to deliver milk, Hurst?"

"I've already explained that, sir."

"Well, explain it again, to save any possible delay in communications, Hurst."

"I only open the Tollhouse door when Boudicca wants to be let in, sir. That's the cat—"

"You mean the outside door is not locked?"

"Mrs. Cater unlocks it before she goes to the toilet, sir. She is a woman of regular habits and always goes—went—at five to seven. When Boudicca hears the toilet flush, she comes out from the shed where she sleeps for the night. Then it depends whether Mrs. Cater or I gets

—got—to the door first. I've already gone over this, sir, with Sid Bowman and—"

"We'd better have it in writing, all the same."

"I've got to go and sign a statement in Pringle police station when I finish my round, sir."

"PC Bowman told you to do that?"

If so, it was, unusually, one up to Bowman.

"No, sir, Inspector Mosley."

"I beg your pardon? When did you see Inspector Mosley?"

"Just as I was leaving the Tollhouse, sir. He came in and asked Sid Bowman what all the fuss was about."

"And where is Inspector Mosley now?"

"Dunno, sir. He went off somewhere in the village."

Chapter Six

Grimshaw decided to call first on Major Hindle. Apart from the fact that he knew no one else in the village, Hindle had struck him yesterday in the pub as a pragmatic and literate character who was likely to have a pretty shrewd finger on the pulse of Marldale.

To find where Hindle lived he had to ask in the super-market, where his very entry caused something of a know-ing flutter. And a group of opinionated theorists at the check-out were keen to raise their voices for his benefit.

"Mark my word, it will be one of the freaks."

"She used to be in and out of the Old Glasshouse as if it were her second home."

"It was a bad day for Marldale when that lot moved in."

"And she was wanting to move them up here, wasn't she?"

"We wouldn't have been safe in our beds."

"If you ask me, none of us *are*."

Major Hindle lived in a small, neat cottage up the cul-de-sac hill that is known in Upper Marldale, for no reason that anyone can remember, as Tinkler's. Mrs. Hindle (Mrs. *Major* Hindle, as she was known in the village) was a little woman, hoovering in a mob-cap, who behaved as if she was afraid that every word she spoke would turn out to have been the wrong thing to say. The Major, she told Grimshaw, was in his workshop at the back. But he had already come into the house at the sound of Grimshaw's voice. Forced now to abandon yesterday's anonymity, Grimshaw intro-duced himself by his rank and station.

"Well, who'd have thought it? Must say you were on

the ball, old chap—up here asking questions before it happened. Pity you didn't stay on a few hours. Might have been able to put a spoke in someone's wheel. I suppose it *is* foul play—otherwise, obviously, you wouldn't be here."

Grimshaw decided that he must not be too free with information. Hindle was quick to notice his pause before replying.

"Or perhaps it's early days, Superintendent—"

"Can't really say until the pathologist has done his thing. But what I'm here for is anything you could tell me about Mrs. Cater—"

"Bea Cater? Well, of course, we've got to start speaking well of her now, haven't we? Got to say I didn't greatly like the woman, though. Don't know anyone who did. I told you that yesterday, so I must be consistent, mustn't I?"

"What was wrong with her?" Grimshaw asked him.

"Too big for Upper Marldale: that's your truth in a nutshell. Not that anyone in Marldale is prepared to admit that anybody's big, but in this case they've been getting it shoved at them too much of the time. And they haven't liked it."

"Too big in what sense?"

"In every sense. In everything she did. She had to be different—and she had to draw everybody's attention to herself. Let me think of an example. When she first came here—oh, it would be three years ago—it got along the vine before anyone had even seen her that the Old Tollhouse had been taken by a sculptress. She wanted the place because the annexe would make an ideal studio. Has a northern light, which is a good thing for an artist to have. Then there was a hell of a to-do with a special surveyor she called in to make sure the floor would stand up to damned great slabs of marble. Art-school trained: but I ask you—I expect you've been in the place already? Did you notice the thing she's got on her easel at the moment? I saw it at one of her charity coffee mornings. Great big black circle with a few blobs of purple slapped here and there. *Imperial haemorrhoids*, that's what I heard somebody call it. Not that I have anything against art and artists, you understand."

Hindle put on a self-deprecating grin.

"Bit of an artist myself, in my own small way—well, craftsman, anyway."

"Oh?"

"Got to do something as an honest pension-eker-outer."

"Paint yourself, do you?"

"Oh, no—nothing so clever. Make walking-sticks. Don't earn a fortune from them, but manage to sell one now and then, through the Craft Shop. Anyway, I was saying—Marldale's got nothing against painting. In fact, the locals like to see somebody with a brush in their hand, immortalizing one of their cottages or a stretch of hillside. Especially if there's a sheep on it. You're as good as an RA any day of the week in Marldale, if you can paint a sheep. But when it comes to doing a diagram of Nero's piles—"

"I don't go for abstracts much myself," Grimshaw said. "But I've yet to hear of them as a motive for murder."

"Ah, yes, don't get me wrong. I'm just trying to put her together for you. Everything she did, you see, had to be off-beam—off other people's beams, anyway. You know, if she was into something fresh—which happened on the average about once a fortnight—she'd drop it like a hot poker if she found it didn't put her into a minority."

"Like what?"

"Well, there was a footpath that a farmer had tried to close over on Marldale Nab, and she threw herself into that as if no one else in Marldale cared. That's something Marldale didn't like. It was their footpath, not hers, her not having lived here all of three years yet. And when the Parish Council called a public meeting about it, she didn't want to know. If it had been *her* committee, with her stirring it all up—see what I mean?"

"That's still not enough in my book to string her up from a beam."

"Don't get me wrong, Superintendent. I'm not suggesting that. It was you who asked my opinion of the woman—"

"Yes—and I see I couldn't have come to a better source. Sorry I interrupted. Do please go on."

"Then there's the Open University. She has to have a degree. Got that before she came here. Not that I have anything against education, you understand, but is it right for these people to be using public funds to spread left-wing balderdash? And you switch your set on in the morning, hoping to hear the overnight score against the Aussies, and what do you get? A bloody talk about Jane Austen."

"You mean that Mrs. Cater held extreme political views?"

"Oh, good God, no. True blue as they come—though she played around with this that and the other. Greenpeace, Amnesty International, Friends of the Earth—you mention it, she'd been a member of it—for a month or so. But she wouldn't join the Conservative Association—though I'll wager she always voted Tory. So why not sail under her true colours, I ask you?"

"But how are you so certain what her views were?"

"Had to be, didn't they, with her background? You know—leopards, spots and all that stuff."

Grimshaw did not want to admit that he did not know what Beatrice Cater's background was, but he did not have long to wait for Hindle to tell him.

"I mean, her husband—died fifteen years ago, poor devil—a top man in the Foreign Office, Germany, Czech-oslovakia, Warsaw. Well, if you ask me, he was a bit more than an office-wallah. So she must have spent the inside of her life rubbing shoulders with the *corps diplomatique.*"

"You did say yesterday that you thought that this local witchcraft nonsense had to do with politics."

"Local politics, old man—purely local."

"To be precise?"

"To be precise, a field, Superintendent. Known to all and sundry here as Ned Suddaby's—though Ned Suddaby died before Prince Albert did. It belonged to the District Council, who bought it years ago for possible council house development. Well, you know this government's policy on council houses, and who the hell wants any more of them in Marldale? Anyway, they decided to put it on the market and they'd had a bid from one of these private health insurance companies who wanted to build a convalescent home. That got our village red-raggers going—not that there are many of them. This social worker woman who's come to live here, some damned woman who's married to a scientist on the industrial estate in Pringle—and, of course, the redoubtable Priscilla Bladon."

"The chief witch?"

"Well, don't ask me what's going on there, Superintendent. That woman's so damned twisted it's a wonder she can pull her stockings on. But these three tried to call a protest meeting to get something done about Ned Suddaby's. Said they wanted it for a playing-field. What do we want in Marldale with a playing-field? And especially on Ned Suddaby's? If they tried to play football there, the uphill team would have to wear crampons. And as for cricket, I doubt whether they could find a wicket from which the batsman could see the bowler. Anyway, nobody went to this meeting except those three, and the convalescent home deal looked as if it was going to go through. Till Madame Cater discovered that here was an act that she wasn't in on. So she started bruiting it abroad that the sale of Ned Suddaby's had never been put out to tender in the proper way. She wanted to put in a bid to build a hostel on it, so that she could move in all that rag, tag and bobtail who are living in squalor in the old military detention camp down in Lower Marldale. And I must say, I can't think of a more appropriate place for them than a glasshouse. I don't know where she thought she was going to raise the money. She talked about getting a grant from the Arts Council, a contribution from Shelter and God knows where else. I'd like to think that nobody would offer her a penny. But the Council had to take her seriously, because there was some doubt on a technicality as to whether this tendering business had been done quite according to Hoyle. So although nobody believed for a moment that she was going to raise the funds for her damned hostel, she gummed up the works as far as the sale to the insurance company was concerned—at least for the time being."

"And for that matter, I suppose, she gummed up the playing-field?"

"Nobody cared two hoots about the playing-field, except Priscilla Bladon and company."

"So Miss Bladon really has gone over the top, as the saying goes."

"You could put it that way."

"I'd better have a little chat with Miss Bladon."

"Well—take a tip from me, Superintendent. She's a difficult woman—very difficult indeed. And she has a stronger hold over a lot of people in this place than you'd think. Before you go and see her, have a word with a friend of yours. He's been handling her for years."

A friend of his? Grimshaw waited for it with introspective dread. Was it possible for him to move anywhere among these hills without someone implying an invidious comparison between himself and Mosley—his underling? He waited for the name to be uttered.

"It's funny: everything I've just said to you, I said to Jack Mosley an hour ago," Hindle said.

"An hour ago?"

"Oh, yes—an early riser, Mosley. He bought a walking-stick, too."

Chapter Seven

Grimshaw came back down the hill known as Tinkler's and stood for a moment looking up and down the Upper Marldale High Street. It was a sunless day, but not an oppressively grey one: a day without highlights—but also, effectively, without shadows. And it was a day with marginally more activity than yesterday afternoon. A knot of four women who had finished their shopping had remained to confer on the pavement outside the supermarket. The man whom Grimshaw had seen wheeling a rabbit-hutch on his bicycle was now coming from the opposite direction, apparently taking his hutch elsewhere.

Grimshaw looked up and down in search of Mosley. Mosley was in this village somewhere, sitting with his raincoat on in the armchair of someone overjoyed to see him; someone who would be pouring vital information into his ears. Grimshaw had not forgotten that by rights Mosley ought to be functioning in Bradburn at this hour. The collation of questionnaires and the logging of the town's nightbirds ought to be complete by now. Mosley ought to be combing through their statements for suggestive discrepancies. Or—Grimshaw had known it to happen—he might be sitting in the refreshment bar on Bradburn bus-station accidentally overhearing one man say to another something innocent and unintentioned that would send him strolling in leisurely fashion among the back-streets to make an arrest.

Grimshaw had not been to his office this morning, and wondered what might have happened in Bradburn last night. Would there have been another mugging? They did not happen every night, but when they did, they generally

happened in threes, in different parts of the town. The
description of the attacker was always the same, for he wore
the shiny plastic mask of a festival clown, and the evil,
expressionless mirth in his painted eyes was almost always
the cruellest part of the trauma in the sick memories of his
victims.

Mosley ought to be in Bradburn—and he was somewhere in Upper Marldale, leaving his Bradburn flank exposed. This time Mosley had overdone it. This time, when
Grimshaw got hold of him, there was going to be no compromise. It was going to be a disciplinary board for Mosley.

But Mosley was nowhere in sight. Grimshaw scanned
the High Street again, now in search of Sergeant Beamish.
Beamish, Grimshaw had told himself, in an epigrammatic
moment that he had had no one to share with, was the
nearest approach to a detective that he had in his force.
Beamish was abrasive, conceited, impossibly well-informed
about techniques in use in other forces, always regretting
the lack of computerized devices that Bradburn could not
afford. Beamish clearly believed that most of the appointments between his own and that of the Chief Constable
were filled by men with straw in their hearts, cotton-wool
in their craniums and water in their veins. Beamish wore
out senior officers to whom he was attached. But Grimshaw
prided himself that he knew how to handle him.

Beamish was eager. Beamish took it as a sign of weak-
ness to be given an order which he could not say he had
already carried out. And the moment the instruction reached
D Division that he was to report to Upper Marldale, he
would be halfway there. But the young man getting out of
the green vintage MG which he had just parked prettily in
the miniature square turned out not to be Beamish.

Then Grimshaw had an inspiration—one of those sub-
tleties of approach that mark out the leaders from the plod-
ders. The obvious thing to do next was to call on Miss
Priscilla Bladon. But men did not become Detective-
Superintendents by dropping mindlessly into the obvious.
Miss Bladon was clearly as strong a character as she was
misguided, and Grimshaw knew, when the truth was crys-
tallized out, virtually nothing about her. Moreover, it was

more than likely that Mosley was closeted with her at this very moment. Well: Mosley could wait. Grimshaw's best plan would be to enter the witches' coven at a level lower than the top, to get his first scrapings of information from one of the less dominant characters. That would enable him to tackle Miss Bladon from a position of strength.

There was Ms. Deirdre Harrison, social worker, but it was hardly likely that she would be in Upper Marldale in the middle of the morning. She would be out somewhere—probably down in the old military detention camp, persuading the undeserving to apply for supplementary benefits that the country could not afford. That left Mrs. Susan Bexwell, housewife, married to an industrial research chemist, and very probably involved in the Bladon set-up only through the desperate boredom of having been brought to live in this world's end. Grimshaw went into the small sub-post-office and asked to see the Electoral Roll: another of the hallmarks of senior experience. He knew that to ask for Mrs. Bexwell by name would be to set up rumours that could make her life misery for weeks: Grimshaw was excelling himself this morning.

The Bexwells lived in one of the newer, detached houses for the prosperous that Grimshaw had observed yesterday. Its garage door was up and over, and he saw that it had its own inspection pit and that the work-bench and tool-rack alongside one wall were the acme of orderliness, with the space for each implement marked with Dymo tape. Two kayak-type canoes were strung up to the rafters. Paddles and an outboard motor were neatly lashed to the wall. Grimshaw also took note of a Flymo, a grass-edge trimmer, a lawn-spiker and every attachment to an electric drill known to DIY man.

From within the house, he heard music—or, at least, the thumping bass accompaniment to music: such melody-line as penetrated to the outside world was too thin to be discernible. Susan Bexwell came to the door: a woman in her late twenties with straw-blonde hair drawn tightly on top and clipped into a pony-tail that hung to her waist. She had on a roll-necked maroon mohair jumper and her legs were encased in white twill trousers that fitted so tightly that it must have been a daily contortion putting them on.

The hall was littered with pull-along, push-along toys, tricycles, a milkfloat four feet high, a model filling-station and two children under five. The melody was more than audible now. It appeared to consist solely of the words *Out of bed, out of mind*, repeated in machine-gun fashion by a voice that reminded Grimshaw of the old one about the man who fell off Sidney Harbour Bridge.

"Detective-Superintendent Thomas Grimshaw, Police Headquarters, Bradburn."

"Yes?"

No element of surprise, even less of welcome; one might say a total lack of interest.

"I'd like to ask you a few questions, if I may."

"I can't think what about."

Grimshaw wondered if in the isolation of her family life it was possible that she had not heard what had happened in the Old Tollhouse.

"You know Beatrice Cater, I believe."

"I have met her."

"You have not heard what has happened to her?"

"I have heard what is said to have happened to her. It's hardly likely that anyone in Upper Marldale has not heard that by now."

She could hardly have been less moved if *Readers' Digest* had selected her to receive six lucky numbers.

"I would like to talk to you about Mrs. Cater, please."

"I don't see to what purpose. I hardly knew her."

"And about one or two other matters."

She resigned herself to his insistence.

"I take it that you have some ID?"

He produced his warrant card, the contents of which she read twice.

"You'd better come in, I suppose."

It was an L-shaped living-room, one wing of which was a dining-area. The floor was laid out with traffic intersections on printed cloth and a fleet of miniature model cars was lying about all over the place. A fairly new baby was tightly wrapped in a carry-cot on a sofa. Mrs. Bexwell had evidently been working at the table. She had books open on it, a pocket calculator with recondite scientific facilities and a pad of A4 refill paper on which she had been doing sprawl-

ing calculations. Grimshaw had sufficient nodding acquaint-
ance with higher mathematics to recognize the differential
calculus. Another acute case of Open University?

"I'm sorry to interrupt your studies," Grimshaw said.

"It doesn't matter. I'm only trying to keep my hand
in."

Out of bed, out of mind—

She went over and turned the volume down a little.

"I really can't think why you should come to me."

"Has anyone else been to see you this morning?"

Fishing for Mosley—

"No. Why should they?"

She looked genuinely puzzled. Despite her aggressive
manner, she was nervous.

"What can you tell me about Mrs. Cater?"

"Nothing. But nothing."

There was a framed enlargement on the wall of a young
woman shooting rapids in a slalom.

"You did tell me you'd met her."

"As I've also met the man who reads the electricity
meter. I could tell you nothing at all about his immortal
soul."

"Were you surprised to hear this morning's news about
Mrs. Cater?"

"Surprised? Yes: I suppose I was. I'd be surprised if
you told me it was half past eleven when it's only half past
ten. Sorry—yes. Of course I was surprised. I'd go so far as
to say shocked. I've never before lived in circles where
people either hang themselves or get themselves hanged."

"But don't you feel involved?"

"Definitely uninvolved."

Out of be-e-d—out of mi-i-i-ind—

There was an outbreak of infantile civil warfare in the
hall. Mrs. Bexwell showed no thought of going to intervene.

"Mrs. Bexwell, I'll not beat about the bush. It has been
mentioned to me that you have been concerned, with one
or two other ladies in the village—"

"Oh, that—strictly for amusement only, Mr. Grimshaw. That's what palmists and crystal-gazers have to say
about themselves on fairgrounds, isn't it?"

"Some people call it witchcraft, Mrs. Bexwell."

"I know. Pathetic, isn't it? We are within the law, Mr. Grimshaw. We are not fraudulent mediums. I do not think there is anything else that you could get us for."

"Mrs. Bexwell, I know perfectly well that you and your friends have done nothing that is not susceptible of a rational explanation."

"I should bloody well hope you do. Otherwise I would wonder why you occupy your present position. And I'm afraid this escapes me: what have the minor amusements of three women on Friday evenings got to do with an unhappy, disorientated, not to say neurotic old woman who created her own half-baked fantasy then couldn't live up to it?"

That, of course, Grimshaw knew, was the key question. That was what he was here to find out—and it was clear that this spitfire mathematician was not going to tell him. But it was not lost on him that in her bad temper she had just come out with a promising mouthful about Mrs. Cater that he was going to have to get her to develop. But before he could start reasoning with her, the doorbell rang again and she got up suddenly from her chair—nerves again— and trod painfully on a vintage Brooke Bond tea van.

"Bugger it!"

She went through the hall, speaking impatiently to one of her children who was in her way. Grimshaw heard a man's voice at the front door, and Mrs. Bexwell was greeting him in a very different tone than she had used up to now.

"Why, hullo—do come in—"

Mosley—Mosley taking off his homburg, revealing the few long strands that he tried to keep plastered across his bald dome. Mosley—by God, no!—actually taking off his raincoat. Mosley in that disgusting navy-blue suit whose pockets were so full that by keeping it buttoned he made himself look like something off a kids' Fifth of November trolley.

"I dare say that you know Mr. Grimshaw," Susan Bexwell said.

"We have met."

"Mr. Mosley will forgive my surprise at seeing him

here," Grimshaw said. "I was under the impression that he was in danger of being overworked in Bradburn."

Mosley affected not to have heard that.

"Coffee, Mr. Mosley?"

"I'd love some."

"And you, Mr. Grimshaw?"

"If it's not too much trouble."

"By the way, Sue," Mosley said. "You can tell Andrew that I tried a packet of those caviare-flavoured crisps. Not bad. Not bad at all. Mind you, he can't lose, can he? How many crisp-eaters know what caviare tastes like? It's lump-fish roe you get in the little pots in the delicatessen."

He turned to inform his superior officer.

"Susan's husband works for Flavour Control. They supply synthetic essences for exotic foodstuffs. Crayfish Crunchies. Squid Nibbles. Shark's Fin Licks. That sort of thing. Sweet things, too—Passion Fruit Suckers."

"Sounds to me as if it's the public who are the suckers."

"Oh, I don't know. People are getting to try stuff that they'd never had put their tongues to in a lifetime. Think of the extension of the public taste," Mosley said. "It's going to be interesting to see whether all this leads to demands for the real thing."

Was Mosley's sense of proportion really such that he thought events in Marldale warranted a protracted conversation about Passion Fruit Suckers and Squid Nibbles? Mrs. Bexwell went to make the coffee, and—poor woman!—Mosley announced that he would help her. Grimshaw heard the pair of them laughing in the kitchen. And then the hatch rattled up and Mosley was looking into the room at him like something out of a comic puppet show.

"I've forgotten how you like yours, Tom."

Tom. Mosley and Grimshaw belonged to an old school, and over two lifetimes, it had only been on rarely emotional occasions that Mosley had used his Superintendent's first name. What was he trying to do? Impress this Bexwell woman?

They came back into the living-room. Susan Bexwell now looked relaxed. For the first time, Grimshaw saw that she was an extremely attractive woman.

"I'm sorry I missed your coven yesterday," Mosley

said. "I got tied up with a bit of bother they've been having in Bradburn. How did things go?"

"Very well. Four of the general public turned up. We put on quite an impressive little act for them."

"And what else is cooking?"

"We're going to have a go at Herbert Garside."

"About time too."

Mosley laughed; and then thought he ought to condescend to put his D-S into the picture.

"Herbert Garside is a farmer who has tried to close a footpath that's been a right of way since the twelfth century. The Parish Council got it open again, of course, but now he's re-routed his cows from the pasture to shippon and has taken to hosing down the track before and after they've passed, so that the path is virtually unusable anyway. So you think you've found a way of getting at old Herbert, do you, Susan?"

"Yes. Hadley Dale Sheep Dog Trials, next Saturday. He stands to win with Sal's Lad, but he isn't going to. In fact he's going to be made to look an ass."

"That'll hit him where it hurts. But watch it, Sue. No harm to animals."

"There'll be no harm to animals, I promise you. And Mr. Mosley—pass the word on where you can, will you? You know what publicity means to us. Everybody's got to know that we've forecast this one."

"I'll do my best. And now, Mrs. Susan Bexwell—to more serious matters."

"Yes, Mr. Mosley."

"You'll have heard what happened to Beatrice Cater?"

"Roughly. Was it murder?"

"Undoubtedly."

"Who'd do that, for God's sake?"

"That's not going to be easy. It's going to keep some of us busy for quite a time. It isn't *knowing* that's going to be the trouble—it's getting enough to bring a man to court. And there are a couple of things I think you can help us with."

Susan Bexwell was now sitting at the table, casting her eye down at her mathematical scrawl without seeing it.

"I can't think what they might be. But I'll try."

"There was a midnight party at the Old Tollhouse last night. Four people. Coffee and green chartreuse."

"I wonder who that can have been?"

"Susan, the pressure's going to be on. The facts are going to come out. Nobody can move about in Marldale by day or night without somebody knowing: even witches. You're going to have to admit it sooner or later. And if you deny it now and have to admit it later, you're going to be in an unenviable position. People like Detective-Superintendent Grimshaw are going to get uptight. He could hold you for questioning for quite a long time."

"We were there," she said.

"What time?"

"We arrived about eleven, left at a quarter to midnight."

"And if Beatrice Cater brought the chartreuse out, I can only think that things must have taken an up-turn between your lot and her."

"She invited us. She'd spotted common interest at last. But it shocks me that—"

"Now you know how right Priscilla Bladon has been all along. One more question. Somebody shared Beatrice Cater's bed last night—or for part of the night. Who?"

"There are limits to my clairvoyance, Mr. Mosley—"

"Bill Hindle?"

"Probably. He's been in the habit for some time. Yes—that would figure. That poor little wife of his thinks that he drinks late at the Crook. Well, he does. So he probably wouldn't have got to the Tollhouse till after twelve. And he daren't stay out all night. I believe he normally gets home about two. I think I might be able to check that for you—or have it checked."

Mosley finished his coffee, collected up their cups and carried them out into the kitchen, where they heard him running water.

"There's no need for you to do that, Mr. Mosley."

"The least I can do. And I shall have to be off. I have other calls to make, as you can imagine."

As soon as they were outside the house, Grimshaw stood and looked at Mosley. He looked at him as a sea-

angler might look at some emaciated, spiny and unidentified
fish that he has brought up when he thought he was into a
codling. Mosley looked back at him utterly unmoved, totally
without feeling—and, an uninformed observer might have
said, absolutely devoid of intelligence.

"Get into my car, Mosley!"

Mosley did that, sliding the passenger-seat forward to
accommodate his short little legs with the maximum comfort. Grimshaw drove them about fifty yards along the road
then stopped and switched off the engine.

"Mosley—why aren't you in Bradburn?"

"There's been a murder in Marldale," Mosley said with
childlike simplicity.

"Mosley, please don't add insolence to insubordination. My orders were plain. There was a sizeable squad put
at your disposal to handle all those questionnaires. I took
men off their rest days to help you. There is a situation in
Bradburn that has people afraid to go out of their own front
doors at night. And here you are, fifteen miles away, in
Marldale."

"Things are going to be tricky up here," Mosley said.

"I'm not interested in what's going on up here," Grimshaw said, then realized that this was the last thing on earth
that he wanted to say.

"You know what I mean, Mosley."

"No, sir."

A shadow appeared to have fallen across the driver's
side-window.

"Mosley—I'm not going to overlook this. This time
you've gone too far. You're on a fizzer, Mosley. I'm hauling
you up before the Chief. I'm going to say that I cannot
continue to be responsible for a Department that has you
in it."

The shadow outside the window deepened. A man's
figure bent down. Grimshaw saw that he was looking up
into Beamish's face.

"Ah. Beamish!"

"Morning, sir. Morning, Mr. Mosley."

Grimshaw looked at him as if he were committing an
offence by taking cognisance of Mosley.

"Sir, I have an urgent message for you from the Assistant Chief Constable. He wants you to go back to Bradburn and report to him."

"Yes, well, I'll give him a ring. It's quite obvious that I'm needed here. I'll see him as soon as I get back—whenever that is."

"He told me to emphasize, sir, that he considers this interview of over-riding importance."

Beamish was looking at Grimshaw rather as Jeeves used to look at his master's erring taste in socks.

"But good God, doesn't he know what I'm up here for?"

"I gathered, sir, that what he wants to see you about has an important connection with what you are up here for."

"But good heavens, Beamish—I've only just got here. I can't start a murder enquiry and then leave it within the first hour."

"I think that thought occurred to the Assistant Chief, sir. He did remark that he had every confidence as long as Mr. Mosley was on the ground."

Something odd seemed to be happening to the landscape. Trees and houses appeared to be about to dissolve like the end of a cinematographic sequence.

"I'm sorry, Sergeant Beamish. I don't think I can have heard you aright. The Assistant—Chief—Constable expressed confidence in Mosley?"

Never mind that Mosley was sitting there, and that Beamish was a junior.

"There hasn't been a change of Assistant Chief Constable since I was last in the office, has there?"

"No, sir."

Beamish's tone could be devastatingly ingenuous when he was delivering a broadside.

"No, sir. But I think he was impressed by Mr. Mosley's performance in Bradburn last night, sir."

"Maybe he was impressed by the very fact that Mosley was in Bradburn at all last night," Grimshaw said. "Go on, Beamish. I'll buy it."

"Well, it seems, sir, that Mr. Mosley took over the file

of old questionnaires at half past five yesterday afternoon, spotted something anomalous and by seven o'clock had been out to their homes and come in with the three Bradburn muggers."

"*Three* Bradburn muggers?"

"Yes. But they only had one mask between them, sir. That's one of the things that has been complicating matters."

"Mosley—why didn't you tell me about this?"

"We seem to have had other things on our plate," Mosley said.

"Mosley, if I were to say to you, I am going to leave you in charge of the Upper Marldale end until I come back, don't do anything controversial and for goodness' sake don't make any statements to the media or the public: what would you do next?"

"I would go down to the former military detention centre, still vulgarly known as the Glasshouse."

"And what would you do there?"

"Among other things I would be looking for some appropriate article of wood carving to give as a coming-of-age present to a niece of mine. There is some very fine workmanship going on down in Lower Marldale—in not the most salubrious of conditions."

"I'll take your word for it. Your fine piece of workmanship would also be a latch-lifter, I take it—a way in: an opportunity to find things out while talking about something quite different."

"I do sometimes find that that works."

"You had better go to it, I suppose. Sergeant Beamish, go with him, and remind him occasionally of standard procedures. And Mosley: I don't care if you picked up thirty Bradburn muggers: I still hate the bloody sight of you."

Chapter Eight

"Just fill me in briefly before we go up to see the Chief."

The Chief. Down among the lower reaches of the force, cynics were sometimes heard to remark that it required an act of faith to believe that there was a Chief Constable. But those who said this knew that they were being less than just. There was indeed a Chief, and those who pretended to deny his existence knew very well that they caught sight of him at regular and predictable if long-drawn-out intervals. The Chief was benign: his leonine sweep of hair helped him to be. And he could afford to be, since he had a Deputy who, like Jimmy the One on a ship, was responsible to him that the System worked. And he had Assistant Chief Constables, five of them, designated *Admin*, *Uniformed Branch*, *Crime*, *Recruitment*, *Training and Intelligence* and *Supply*, who did everything for him that was difficult, nasty, diplomatically dangerous, unkind—or that might in any other way jeopardize the omni-benevolent image.

"The object of my life is to have nothing to do."

This was one of the Chief's most frequent and credible pronouncements, meaning that having decreed that the System should function, all he had to do was to sit back and let it do so, every cog sweetly lubricated and content to be playing its perhaps insignificant part.

"Though in point of fact we are all human. An occasional minor intervention is not to be avoided, and oddly I do seem to find myself working an eighteen-hour day, seven days a week."

"By which," ACC (A) was once reported to have said to ACC (R, T & I), "one is led to believe that he considers himself to be working as long as he is making the effort to remain clinically awake."

But an intervention by the Chief on a case in progress was momentous. Detective-Superintendent Grimshaw could not remember when it had last happened to him. He believed that it had been back in the Crippsian austerity of 1949, when a County Council clerk had had to be charged with taking home paper-clips and a rubber eraser from Office Services. One of the reasons for Grimshaw's prolonged good standing had been his bright suggestion in committee that the said clerk be persuaded to say that he had taken the materials in order to do unpaid overtime in his own sitting-room.

And *Just fill me in briefly*—that was the other thing that the ACC (Crime) had said. Grimshaw had expected that and had applied some mental activity to it during his drive back to Bradburn.

A contrary cat called Boudicca who declined to the point of an arched back to enter her home; a graduate sexagenarian who had managed to go to bed with a man, as yet unknown, between a dormitory feast and getting herself strung up to a beam; a plot of dead cabbages that had seemed so sinister that *Mosley—Mosley*—had referred them to Forensic; a farmer who had made a slough of a public footpath; Squid Nibbles; Passion Fruit Suckers; a forthcoming threat—nay, a promise—to nobble a sheepdog called Sal's Lad at a trial: an operation, incidentally, that was to be given the maximum publicity, and to which a Detective-Inspector of this force was lending spontaneous encouragement.

"I'm not quite in a position to pull all the threads together yet."

"But you do have clues?"

"Any amount of them."

"The Chief is bound to want a rapid *tour d'horizon*."

It was a prospect that would have worried Grimshaw more if he had had more time to think about it. As it was he was not able to speak again before the ACC had whisked him up the sanctified stairs, had muttered the password-of-the-day to the undoubtedly armed stenographer on duty and had opened the door for him to walk into the Chief's most radiant smile.

"Ah. Detective-Superintendent Grimshaw!"

The Chief seemed to regard this as a very satisfying feat of memory.

"All well with you I hope, Grimshaw? That lad of yours get his O Levels?"

"He completed his Ph.D last summer," Grimshaw said. "Just been interviewed by Tesco's—job sticking price-labels on tins."

"Well, there's nothing like practical experience. And how are the Lutinos?"

"Lutinos, sir?"

"You're thinking of Chief Inspector Walsh, sir," the ACC said. "He's the one who breeds the budgerigars."

"Ah. Well, you seem to be having an exciting time up in Marldale, Grimshaw."

"Fairly eventful, sir."

"If you could just give me a quick *tour d'horizon*."

To his surprise, Grimshaw heard himself supplying a reasonable summary.

"A woman's been murdered. We're waiting for the path lab to confirm that it is murder, and perhaps to supply helpful details that aren't in our capacity to detect. The issue is complicated, and yet may ultimately be explained, by a wave of the sort of silliness that affects these rural communities from time to time."

"You mean witchcraft?"

"Of a kind."

"And Mosley has everything firmly within his grasp?"

"He appears to have."

He wasn't going to fall out over an adverb like *firmly*, and it would not have been appropriate at this stage to mention the consolation of having Beamish on the ball.

"Marvellous job Mosley did over those Bradburn yobbos."

"I haven't had time to read the detailed case-report yet, sir."

"Mosley went through the questionnaires like a wire through cheese. Spotted triangular movements, reported by neighbours: A to B's house, B to C's, then C back to A's. Mosley happened to know the laddies concerned. Realized that this was how they were passing the mask on,

one to the other. Went out singly and walked them back
one at a time to the station."

"Well, it's easy for Mosley. He knows an awful lot of
people," the ACC said.

"Well, now—the reason I'm making such inroads into
your time, Grimshaw, is to show you this—"

He opened a drawer, brought out a file, examined it
briefly to see that it was the right one, and passed it over
the desk. Not sure whether he was meant to read it all
through on the spot, Grimshaw glanced at the top sheet.
It was addressed to *Dick*, signed *Tod*, and appeared to mean
nothing at all.

"I'll cut the corners for you, Grimshaw. A little over
a year ago the Chief Executive Officer of the County Council
referred papers to the Director of Public Prosecutions: well,
not to the DPP himself. He has a friend in the Director's
office who was prepared to give a non-committal unofficial
opinion. What one has to call the unacceptable face of pri-
vatization. I fear that in any organization, however right-
eously administered, there are always some who seek to
operate their responsibilities to their private advantage.
Otherwise we three also, of course, might be earning our
bread sticking on price-tags in supermarkets."

Witticism of the morning—duly appreciated by a discreet chuckle. The Chief continued.

"Three County Councillors—at least three, cutting
across party lines—are believed to be involved—and, I
regret to say, more than one permanent servant of the
Council that we ourselves serve."

He allowed this outrageous proposition time to take
root.

"Unfortunately the man in the Prosecutor's has said
that there is insufficient evidence on which he can take
action. You will understand, of course, that the DPP is
not guided by his private opinions about anyone's guilt,
but solely by the probability of success in the courts. The
official line would have to be that with the case as it stands,
the culprits would come away laughing, the name of this
authority would have been dragged through the mud over
a period of months, and the helpless British tax-payer

would have to foot the bill for the legal costs of both sides."

Déjà vu—

"The CEO of the CC has however been to London to talk to the DPP's assistant. 'Those men are villains,' that's what his friend said to him. And he went on to suggest the nature of additional evidence which, if forthcoming, would go a long way towards clinching the case. That's where you come in, Grimshaw. Or, rather, that's where you don't come in."

Thanks for the clarity—

"You see, one of the leading lights, perhaps *the* leading light, in this private cornering of what were previously public assets, is undoubtedly County Councillor Whitcombe."

Harry Whitcombe—a genial type. He had tried to ply Grimshaw with pints, once when the D-S was talking to Rotary.

"Now Councillor Whitcombe came to see me last week, telling me alarming stories of things that are alleged to be going on in Marldale, and pleading with me to find a way through the law to suppress the activities of these self-styled witches. The reason he gave for his concern was the unrest that they are causing throughout the length of the valley."

Harry Whitcombe had been in to see the Chief? But Grimshaw thought that it had been Beatrice Cater who had laid a complaint. Ah, no: he saw now how it must have been. Beatrice Cater had been fobbed off with the ACC, but it was impossible to fob Councillor Whitcombe off with anyone.

"The lady who died last night, Mrs. Cater, also came to these offices recently. She told a story so obscure, so confused and so intricate—"

"And repetitive," the ACC inserted.

"—that one can only admire the dedication of the man who had to listen to it."

Pause for the ACC and the Chief to smile endearingly at each other.

"The point I am coming to is that Mrs. Cater seemed to think that in some manner about which she found it difficult to be explicit, the caperings of these witches have to do with the sale of a field belonging to the Pringle and

Marldale District Council, for which various bodies have
suggested uses. Councillor Whitcombe is also a member of
the Pringle Council, but we have so far been unable to see
how he could be a beneficiary from the sale of the field. So
what we are proposing to do now is this, Grimshaw—"

The Chief looked all round himself, to ensure that there
were no spies in the room.

"Leave the solution of the murder entirely to Mosley:
though I suggest that you give him some reinforcement.
Why not bring up that sergeant, what was his name, Beamish, from one of your divisions? They've worked very well
together before. And do not, under any circumstances, say
anything to either of them about our broader suspicions.
We do not want Mosley going anywhere near Councillor
Whitcombe. One of the reasons I am suggesting Mosley for
the job is that he is painstaking—and slow. With Mosley
taking his time over every clod of earth in Marldale, and
Beamish rooting up ingenious cross-trails all over the place,
it will give us time, you see—time for you, Superintendent
Grimshaw, to get to work, in close collaboration with our
colleague here, to see what you can dig out at the Bradburn
end. It will probably mean close scrutiny of several years
of Council and Committee minutes. And I need hardly say
that you have a direct line to me while this investigation
lasts. In fact, I would be obliged, Superintendent, if you
would regard me as personally directing this enquiry. It
would be better if you did not take any positive step without
consulting me first."

Grimshaw went back to his office and waited for normal
clarity of consciousness to return. Then he picked up a sheaf
of papers that his sergeant-clerk had laid where they could
not fail to catch his eye. There were a few preliminary
reports from Forensic about some of the items that Scene
of Crime had brought in. Black canine hairs, for one thing.
And a smear taken on cotton-wool from a pane of glass in
the studio-annexe of the Old Tollhouse, Upper Marldale,
had been identified as Windowlene.

Chapter Nine

The orientation that Mosley offered Beamish as the sergeant drove them down to Lower Marldale was by no means as succinct as some of the explanations that had been exchanged in the Chief's office. For one thing there were interruptions. Beamish was called on to stop more than once: to examine the painted cabbalistic sign on the back of a sheep, which Mosley suspected of having been rustled; to examine the debris of a picnic—and to clear up the litter into a plastic bag in Beamish's boot; and once simply to admire the scenery, where a low-hanging cloud was clinging to the flank of a green clough.

"So really, you're on the side of these three women," Beamish said.

"They are honest and diligent strivers after something."

"One at least of them must be pretty clever. There are things that don't exactly explain themselves."

"Having difficulty, are you?"

"Some. These cats, for example. Don't think for a moment, Mr. Mosley, that I hesitate to take your word for anything you've told me. But here we have—and you tell me that you have carefully cross-checked the evidence—a community of cats who refuse to leave their home premises—and yet one solitary exception among cats goes out and does just the opposite. She refuses to cross the doorstep that at one time must have represented all she wished for in the way of warmth, food and cosseting. Now if you were to ask me to get cats to behave like that, I'd have to take advice."

"Really? It would depend on who you knew."

"How come?"

"Lion piss," Mosley said. "That's what they've been using."

"Easy to come by in these parts, is it?"

"It is if you're married to a man who can make Chitterling Chews, Rhino Horn Bitters and Larkspur Lollies. I happen to know that Flavour Control, Ltd. do not limit their activities to the taste-buds. They also cater for the olfactory nerve. An after-shave lotion that makes a man smell horsy. A spray which if applied behind the ears will render any woman irresistible to a Pekingese. No need therefore to import the urine of the greater cats direct from the savannah."

"You think that's how it was done, do you?"

"Something like that. Some sort of synthetic essence. I tremble to think what's going to happen to Sal's Lad at the Hadley Dale Trials. If he should mistake one of the sheep for a bitch of his own species on heat—"

"You think this could be done, do you?"

"I'm sure it could. I once went to a zoo, Sergeant Beamish, where a woman had been so scatter-brained as to introduce a small domestic pet under cover of her coat. A spry little Schipperke, he was, and when she got him into the Large Cat House, he nearly did his nut, catching the message of smells outside the range of human perception. God knows what the little dog thought was going to happen to him. And I'm quite sure that Mrs. Susan Bexwell, as the party was leaving the Old Tollhouse after Beatrice Cater's liqueurs, took the opportunity of doctoring the doorway. I hope so, anyway, because Susan Bexwell does not strike me as a woman devoid of good taste, and if the trio had had anything to do with executing Mrs. Cater, she'd never have played a practical joke as non-U as that. Oh—they're a bright little bunch of vigilantes, have no doubt. My only fear is that their efforts are going to be discouraged before they have broken this case for us."

"You mean they're going to take fright?"

"Not of us, Sergeant Beamish. But last night's goings-on are going to bring the press here. I can picture the cellars of the Crook being drained dry at this moment by young

men and women accompanied by cynical photographers.
And in the Crook they are going to hear sundry stories.
The witches of Marldale are going to get more publicity
than they will care for. We shall have to keep a close eye
on them. The last thing on earth we want is for them to
suspend their campaign: whatever it's about."

They stopped talking as they ran down into the village.
Lower Marldale was only about a fifth of the size of its more
highly placed neighbour and did not look as if it was considered worth a tenth of the care. It lacked any domestic
building later than Edwardian and there was nothing to try
to live up to. It was not just that the paintwork of too many
of the houses was a decade overdue for renewal. It was not
that too many curtains needed to be taken down and washed.
It was not merely that, unlike Upper Marldale, the village
had no pavements. These things were all true, but it was
untidiness that gave the place its dismal air. A public waste-
bin, filled to overflowing by last season's tourists, had not
been emptied: it would be, perhaps, before next Easter.
There were cola tins lying squashed in the main street and
rutted tyre-marks proclaimed the use of the green as a casual
car park.

But even this seemed cheerfully civilized by comparison with the next vista towards which Mosley told Beamish
to drive. The land flattened out at the bottom end of the
valley, losing the relief of rolling flanks and now occupied
largely by the widening of the river, which had grown
sluggish and held in suspension the milky residue of some
rurally sited industry. And by the water's edge was a can-
tonment of army huts, many of their windows boarded over,
their guttering sprung, some of the doors missing and a pile
of domestic rubbish, including stinking rags, smouldering
lethargically on a corner of the one-time parade ground.
Here and there round the perimeter were rusty remnants
of triple-coiled barbed wire.

"Imagine the abandonment of hope by all who entered
here," Mosley said.

"They were criminals," Beamish reminded him.

"Military criminals—which means you could wind up
in a place like this by sheer bad luck; or by being so hard-

pushed that you forgot to hold your tongue. Can you picture wintering here, Beamish?"

One or two of the hut chimneys were giving out smoke. A few people had made a braver show with curtains than some of the villagers. Some of the occupants had had a go at gardening, edging border beds in the sorry soil with bits of broken tile. Mosley seemed to know his way about the residents, was apparently known to most of them, and resented by none. In one grubby workshop a man was making bamboo pipes of Pan, in another a man and a woman were blowing glass baubles: little elephants and swans. One man sat unhappily behind a stack of unfired ceramics.

"Vicious circle, Mr. Mosley. Can't get the kiln repaired till I've sold this lot. Can't complete this lot till I've had the kiln repaired."

In a woodwork shop, Joe Murray, a man in a butcher's apron, was working at a lathe with a dedicated steadiness that suggested relative success. Mosley spent some time examining his stock.

"I might be back again before we go to buy this salad bowl, Joe. What is it? Walnut?"

"Pear-wood."

"You've certainly made the most of the grain. But I can't make my mind up between wood and pewter. I'll have to go first and see what Richard has to offer."

"Richard's gone. Got a short lease on a lock-up site in Bradcaster."

"Has there been much coming and going recently?"

"One or two casuals. I don't pay much attention these days. They come and go without me noticing."

"How many permanent residents have you now?"

"Thirtyish, give or take a few, and not counting kids. Christ knows how many kids."

"I expect he does," Mosley said. "I've no doubt he keeps some sort of list."

Mosley led Beamish across the former parade square.

"Takes all sorts. There are some good craftsmen here. Others would be misfits in any environment. You've seen enough to know they're not all freaks."

"How well organized?"

"They have a loose sort of constitution, try to protect themselves against trouble-makers. No specific religious tie-up. General morality's a bit come-and-go. Some personalities are obviously stronger than others, but what they've always lacked is effective leadership. Let's see if there's anyone in the office."

He led Beamish across the crumbling asphalt of the square towards a wooden building with a veranda that must once have been the Orderly Room. Now most of its windows were broken, but one sector was in use as an office. There was a notice-board outside the door that flapped with posters relating to DHSS benefits, Legal Aid facilities and slogans for minority causes: anti-vivisection, anti-bloodsports, transcendental meditation.

A man was leaning on the rail of the veranda with the slow-limbed idleness of an extra on a Western film-set. When they came within earshot of the office, they heard a woman's voice raised within its walls.

"Hullo, Mr. Mosley," the man on the rail said. "I'm out again."

"Try and stay out," Mosley said without looking at him.

The woman's voice was short-tempered in the precise but flat vowels of the West Riding, the unvoiced consonants of Bradford.

"If you think you can come to me with a bloody tale like that, you bloody little arsehole-crawler—"

"It helps if you speak the language of the natives," Mosley said.

"I'll tell you what I'm going to bloody do, Cartwright. Jobs are bloody hard to come by and there aren't all that many strings left for even me to pull. But I'm going to do for you the worst that anybody's done for you in years. I'm going to see you into a job, if I have to perjure myself to an employer. Work, Cartwright: it comes to us all in the end. And if you don't sodding well hold this job down, I'll make sure your file gets lost for six bloody months. And I'll tell Mavis where she can find you."

Mosley knocked and pushed the door open. The woman who had been speaking was of deceptive age. She was actually thirty-four, but seen full face and from a short dis-

tance, she could momentarily have looked about sixteen—
an overfed and unco-ordinated sixteen, with a pasty com-
plexion relieved only by acne. Her contours suggested an
exclusive diet of sweetened starches and she was wearing a
bib-and-brace overall in dirty purple corduroy, its shoulder-
straps uneven.

"Did you hear what she said to me, Mr. Mosley?" said
the man to whom she had been speaking.

"Piss off!" she told him.

"Miss Deirdre Harrison," Mosley said. "Local liaison
officer for the Welfare State. That's not the way she always
speaks to her clients. Sometimes she gets quite cross with
them."

"We're not supposed to become emotionally involved,"
she said. "But sometimes—"

"Deirdre, there are one or two bits of things—"

"Yes. I thought there might be."

"The first's a quickie. Casuals in this place—any short-
stay clients within the last week?"

"Don't ask me. I don't bloody well live here, you
know—come in once a week when I can't find an excuse
to go somewhere else."

"No—but they'll tell you more readily than they'll tell
me. You can always pretend you're looking for some character who's due for back-benefit."

"I'll do what I can."

"I need this information fast, Deirdre."

"So where am I going to find you when I've got it?"

"I'll be around your place this evening."

"Bang goes another bloody reputation. You think that
was an outside job, last night, do you, Mr. Mosley?"

"I wouldn't be surprised if there was a contract on Mrs.
Cater. I think that's the current idiom. And that brings me
to my second point. What went on up there last night?"

"It's no use coming to me about that."

"Come off it, Deirdre. We know you were up there
slurping Mrs. Cater's liquor. That fact's out."

"Have you been to see Priscilla?"

"Not yet. Joy to come."

Deirdre Harrison thought for some seconds.

"Come on, Deirdre. I know you'd like the chance to co-ordinate your stories. I've got a rough idea what you three are up to and it's going to face the light of day before so long."

"You're going to bugger it up for us."

"Not if I can help it. How do you know I'm not working on the same thing myself? I do know, by the way, that you went to the Tollhouse on Mrs. Cater's invitation. That means she had something to tell you—for a change."

"God, I hated that woman," Deirdre said.

"I know you did. Feel differently about her now, I suppose?"

"A bit mixed up, Mr. Mosley, to tell you the truth. She's been murdered, and any woman has the right not to be murdered. But she was so bloody false, that's what got on my wheel. Nothing about her was what she cracked it on to be—nothing. And yet she didn't tell lies, you know. She just had a crafty way of causing lies to be thought. Sometimes I think she even believed every latest bit of falseness that she put out."

"Folk have been known to do just that."

"Husband in the Diplomatic Service? Well, I've been through every Whitaker's Almanack since the war, and every Statesman's Year Book, and I can't find him."

"Maybe he was ex-directory."

"And maybe he bloody wasn't. We heard she was a sculptress, didn't we? But when has her studio ever seen a lump of stone? Art College trained? Have you ever seen a specimen of her work? She couldn't put a wash of bloody colour on. She hadn't an inkling of design, of composition, light and shade—*When I was at such-and-such a College*—that's how she drip-fed it out of the side of her mouth. In point of fact, she probably went to an evening class or two on the premises: I'll bet she never completed a course in her life. *In my Open University days*—I heard her say that myself. Meaning what? That she'd watched a few broadcasts, maybe even got as far as sending for a course book. But she can't have had a degree, Mr. Mosley—she can't have! She hadn't the intelligence of a bloody rabbit."

"Maybe so. I know you didn't like her. And I think I

know why you didn't. If ever a couple of women were incompatible, it was you two. But someone's killed her, and as you've just said, we prefer that sort of thing not to happen. And she was killed because of something she knew— something that she'd sent for you three to tell you."

"I wish you'd talk to Priscilla about this."

"I shall be doing."

"Well, take me with you when you do. Let's go now—"

"What is this, Deirdre? *Esprit de corps?* Witches' honour?"

"You don't understand, Mr. Mosley."

"I think I do. Well—I shall have seen Priscilla by the time I come round to see you tonight for that other piece of information. And maybe we'll all end up in Priscilla's sitting-room before the night's out."

Both men were quiet as they drove back up the valley. Beamish was waiting for Mosley to volunteer some commentary on what they had been listening to. Mosley was smoking his pipe to a slow rhythm, saying nothing. The cloud that he had admired on the way down had now drifted lower and was completely obscuring the clough.

"So that's a Social Welfare Officer," Beamish said at last.

"A young lady who has done a great deal of unsung good in her time."

"I don't doubt it."

"But frustrated. Which breaks out now and then. Put yourself in her position, Beamish, in the wake of what's happened."

"Oh, yes, sir—I can see all that. The only thing—"

"Is that you think I let her off too lightly? Let her call the tune?"

"I didn't say that."

"No. But you're excused for thinking it."

"So what have they got on their minds, these three?"

"Nothing that they've cause to be ashamed of. Something that they think is going to be ruined if it falls into our lap before it's ripe. Everything in your manual, Sergeant Beamish, would tell you not to let them confer before you put the pressure on. Everything in my manual tells me that once they've conferred we may not have to use much pressure. Basically they're honest. We mustn't force dishonesty on to them."

They began to climb a series of hairpins that showed them Upper Marldale's roofs and chimneys from a shifting range of angles.

"We'll go and see Priscilla Bladon now. She'll be expecting us. And if you think you've met some characters in the last few hours, they'll have paled into nothingness before you're much older, Sergeant Beamish."

Chapter Ten

Grimshaw cleared his desk and did his best to clear his mind. It meant dropping everything else, and as long as he was in his office, or anyone in his office knew where to find him, that was impossible. Was this why Mosley disappeared from the official ken for days at a time? There were days when Grimshaw found it physically impossible to get on with anything big or new. His working hours were filled with tangential aggro, mostly on the phone, solving other people's problems for them. The first thing was to get hold of Council Minutes for the last few years. And even in asking for the documents, he had to be circumspect. There must not be a whisper in County Hall that CID were showing interest. It was true that the Chief Executive Officer was privy to the enquiry—in fact it had started life as his enquiry—but even CEOs had clerks to handle paper for them. And if anyone in County Hall, democrat or official, had been working a fiddle, it must have been with the connivance of some clerk who was being kept quiet by a proportionate rake-off.

So Grimshaw rang up a friend, a master at the Bradburn Sixth Form College, and persuaded him to beg a set of records for a Civic Studies project. By three in the afternoon they had been delivered to the Superintendent's desk. He picked up the first month's copy—and was immediately called away to deal with a Justice of the Peace who was not happy about a search warrant that he had been asked to sign in a far corner of the territory. Then Bradcaster City Borough were on, asking to borrow anti-pickpocket reinforcements for a forthcoming football match. Grimshaw put the minutes in his briefcase and decided to do the rest of his day's work at home. But not before he had read the first report that had come in from the Scene of Crime squad, together with a cautious and unofficial preliminary from the pathologist.

It was no surprise to learn that Beatrice Cater's neck had been broken by a deeper drop than could have been contrived from her living-room beam. There were abrasions about her wrists and ankles suggesting that at some stage these had been tied. There was no sign of indecent assault. There was a specimen of alien hair about her genitalia, but she had not had intercourse within the last twenty-four hours. Specimens of two people's hair found among her bed-linen were categorically declared to belong neither to Mrs. Cater nor to the other person with whom she had been in close contact. There had even been doggy hairs in the bed.

Inspector Heathcote's team had made discoveries that bore strongly on the pathologist's findings. Scratches in the paintwork of a wooden panel in the ceiling of Mrs. Cater's bedroom, giving access to loft space, indicated that this had been recently moved. A groove cut into the deep dust on a joist pointed to where the rope could well have been made firm. A whitewood table in the studio-annexe, normally used for storing paints and brushes, had been cleared of its contents, and there were scratches in its spatterings of paint that could have been made while it was being used as a hangman's drop. No explanation was attempted as to why the victim had been hanged in one place, then removed to be discovered in a neighbouring room.

Grimshaw had three copies made of these reports and had a motor-cyclist deliver them in places where they were likely to reach Mosley. He also instructed Mosley to establish an Incident Room in Marldale at once. He resisted the temptation to add that if he did not know what an Incident Room was, he could ask Beamish.

Meanwhle Mosley, who had arrived back in Upper Marldale with Beamish, was now showing no urgency about going to see Priscilla Bladon. He seemed in fact to have changed his priorities and now had time to kill. He took Sergeant Beamish up to the Old Tollhouse and turned him loose among the evidence on the spot, which the young man tackled with ardour and system. He found all that the Scene of Crime people had found, and more besides: all the minor damage done to paintwork, the loft-panel and the whitewood table. And all the while that he was searching, noting and deducing, Mosley sat in an armchair in Mrs. Cater's polygonal living-room, with his coat open and his hat pushed back, sucking pensively at an unlit pipe. He was rather like a tired but dutiful father who has taken his children out to play in the woods, and who subsides on to the nearest log to let them get on with it.

Beamish went and carried the table in from the studio, set it under the loft-trap, and from that combination was joyfully able to discover a small tear in the wallpaper at the right height and size to have been made by swinging heels. He raised his voice in excitement as he pointed this out to Mosley, but Mosley behaved for all the world as if other men's eagerness passed him by.

"Whoever did it came equipped with a complete hanging kit."

"Not at all a bad thing to do, if you ever go out on a hanging expedition," Mosley said.

Beamish came up from the carpet with a short length of cotton thread.

"Do you know what this was used for?"

"You have an idea, Sergeant?"

"To tie up a loop so that the noose was hanging at the right height to be slipped over the victim's neck. It would break immediately the rope took her weight."

"Finesse," Mosley said.

"That's the way the official hangman used to do it. I read it in Pierrepoint's *Memoirs*."

"He had had ample opportunity to work out the least troublesome way to set about the job."

"So what sort of a murderer is it who comes out tooled up strictly according to Home Office practice?"

"A man who enjoys his work," Mosley said. "There's one way in which he doesn't seem to have been equipped. There was no linen bag over her head. Do you know why that was, Sergeant Beamish?"

"Can't guess."

"He didn't want to miss the look on her face," Mosley said.

He got up and went to look at one of Mrs. Cater's abstract paintings: a number of unevenly overlapping squares in primary colours. Beamish came and joined him. Neither man ventured an opinion.

"Sergeant Beamish—I think I ought to give you a few preliminary warnings about Priscilla Bladon."

"Yes, sir?"

Perhaps some of the senior officers who found Beamish wearing would have got on better with him if they had learned to tolerate his eagerness. Mosley did not seem to notice it.

"I can't provide you with a formula for dealing with her, Beamish, because there's no telling which version of Priscilla Bladon she'll choose to present to us today. But I know one thing: if she appears irrational—it will be because that's how she wants to appear. But let's go back into town, shall we? It will be interesting to see what strangers have arrived."

Chapter Eleven

"Headmistress of Marldale C of E Primary School for the inside of her life," Mosley said. "Including the days before they used to ship them off to Pringle at the age of eleven. There's a generation in Upper Marldale that received all the education they ever had at the hands of Priscilla Bladon. And it was literally *at her hands*. Take a look at those hands when you see them, Sergeant Beamish. You could picture them fixing a pit-prop. If you got one of those callused old palms round the back of your head with a well-judged arc of follow-through, you left off whatever it was she'd caught you doing."

Mosley nodded through the car window at a man who was pushing a cycle along the Upper Marldale pavement. He was taking a rabbit-hutch somewhere.

"Never trained, of course, but none the less monumental for that. You get half a dozen old pupils of Priscilla's together in a bar—which is likely to be happening at any moment in Marldale, irrespective of licensing hours—and it's a fair bet what the talk will get on to. Take spelling, for example. Very keen on orthography, was Miss Bladon. If a lad got a word wrong more than once, she used to chalk it back to front on the sole of an old plimsoll, on the grounds that if she couldn't work it in at the top, she'd knock it in at the bottom. Hullo! I thought our friend would be turning up."

Mosley was looking back over his shoulder. Beamish could not see who it was that he had spotted.

"And of course, Miss Bladon didn't consider that her responsibilities stopped at the classroom door. And by that I don't mean a stamp-collecting club after four o'clock. If

there was anything affecting a child in her school, then it
became her business at once—and it was remarkable what
did come to her ears. Take Matty Walton. When he was
about six, Matty Walton had a spell of coming late for school,
looked as if he hadn't slept, used to faint during school
prayers. Leave it to Miss Bladon. She soon found out that
the trouble was the terrifying night he always had when his
father came home pie-eyed from the Crook. So she ups and
sees Jenny Walton. Little shrimpy woman she was, scared
stiff of her Arthur, a damned great ox of a man, either
amorous or aggressive or both when he'd had a pot or two.
If she hadn't got him a supper on the table, he used to
throw everything out of all the food-cupboards. If she'd
cooked him a meal, he'd scrape it on to the fire. But then
one night when Arthur came home the worse for wear, he
found two of them waiting for him—only Priscilla hid in
the scullery till he had hold of his wife's wrists and started
shoving her up against the door as if he was making love
to her down some alley. Then Priscilla came up behind and
clouted him two or three times across each ear-hole with
those hands of hers. She put a mark or two on him that he
took to work with him the next morning, then laid him out
cold when she got bored with playing games with him."

Mosley looked again over his shoulder.

"Pull over into Market Square, Beamish. We'll waylay
that young lady."

Beamish still could not see who he was talking about.
He followed Mosley over to the Community Centre, where
they pretended to read the notice-board.

"Another time, young Tommy Haslam sat at his desk
all one day snivelling. Wouldn't for the life of him tell her
what it was about. She couldn't tempt him this way or that
to let on what was going on at home—but she had no
difficulty in prising it out of the neighbours. Tommy Haslam
Senior had gone off to shack up with a barmaid in Bradcaster. So Priscilla Bladon pays Joe Scragg to give her a lift
in one evening on his coal-wagon, and when Joe comes back
three hours later, he has two passengers. Thomas Haslam
hasn't left home ever since. Nobody knows what Priscilla
said or did to him."

Mosley suddenly twisted round to face the pavement. Deirdre Harrison had come shambling up. There seemed something unco-ordinated about her gait: she might from a distance have been taken for a fifth-year secondary-school educationally sub-normal.

"Ah! Deirdre! Come to square up your yarn with Priscilla, have you?"

"It isn't that, Mr. Mosley."

"Did you find out what I wanted to know?"

"That didn't take two minutes."

"Let's have it, then."

There was normally a placidity about Mosley suggesting that all he had to do was to wait for events to explain themselves. But once or twice when they had worked together Beamish had seen a certain nervosity come over him. The signs of it were apparent now. Beamish wondered what Mosley would be like if he actually did become impatient. Maybe it would be no bad thing, once in a while.

"Do you really want us to talk here?"

Deirdre Harrison looked significantly about them, and there were one or two people in the High Street not known by sight either to Mosley or herself. A man in an Arran sweater was talking to a girl in a toggled duffel coat. Across on the other pavement two middle-aged men with telephoto lenses fitted to their cameras were chatting outside the Craft Shop.

"They can't hear us," Mosley said. "And if you could find out in two minutes, you can tell me in less."

"Three punks," she said. "One man, one woman, one indeterminate. Red Indian tonsures. All the trimmings. Age mid-twenties—or could have been drug-raddled adolescents."

"What time was this?"

"About three in the afternoon. Joe Murray booked them in. Officially they should have been vetted by a subcommittee, but that often goes by the board. They've got a basic drill for casual visitors—but all it amounts to is that no one's turned away on their first night, unless they're fighting drunk. After that, it depends on how they fit in."

"And whether they can be got rid of."

Deirdre relaxed enough for a short-lived grin.

"Some of their methods are quite unscrupulous. I've actually heard an undesirable threatened with you."

"That'll be the day. So Joe Murray admitted these three?"

"They said they only wanted one room, and in the Glasshouse people don't ask questions about personal pastimes. He put them in what used to be an NCOs' annexe at the end of one of the huts. And what a bloody night the Glasshouse spent—at least, anybody within earshot of those three. Fighting, swearing, singing, three-ended sex—though which three ends was anybody's guess."

"Till what time?"

"Joe and one or two others went out to read the Riot Act between two and three. They'd locked themselves in, and Joe threatened to set fire to the hut if they didn't pipe down."

"Pity he didn't."

"Well, anyway, that shut them up to some extent. There was one more outbreak of singing—one of them had a guitar—but nothing to complain about by Glasshouse standards."

"And then, came the dawn, they were gone?"

Deirdre looked curiously at Mosley.

"You on to something already?"

"Only what's obvious."

At this moment the man in the Arran sweater came up with the girl in the duffel coat, having beckoned to one of the photographers, who was unbuttoning his camera-case as he crossed the road.

"Miss Deirdre Harrison?"

Even for an outdoor shot he was using electronic flash, wisely for the afternoon murk of Marldale.

"And you must be Inspector Jack Mosley."

Shopkeepers would have been readily helpful to the pressmen. Rather to Beamish's surprise, Mosley co-operated quite meekly and gave the photographer the grouping he wanted. And already other reporters were appearing, like ants busied by the lifting of a stone.

"Are you yet in a position to make a statement?"

"Can you give us a slant on the witchcraft angle?"

"When is the next meeting of your coven, Miss Harrison?"

"Do you seriously think that there is any connection between this killing and twentieth-century black magic, Inspector?"

"May we say that you three ladies are putting your talents at the service of the police?"

"Will you be holding a session in the near future to look into your crystal ball?"

"What would be the official attitude to an offer of help from the ladies, Mr. Mosley?"

"You can quote me as saying that I shall be glad of help from whatever source it is offered."

Beamish sighed. Mosley seemed determined to walk into it.

"Including sorcery?"

"I'll consider everything on its merits," Mosley said.

"Is there any truth in these rumours about the cats?"

"I don't deal in rumours."

"I believe you've carried out several investigations in this town within the last week or so. A cabbage patch. A hen run. Would you like to say whether you think there's any connection?"

"Not until I know."

"Is it true that Miss Cater had been refused admission to the coven?"

"That's a new one on me," Mosley said.

"If it's true, would you say it has any significance?"

"If it's true, I dare say it signifies something."

"Do you see significance in Mrs. Cater's relationships with the inmates of the former Glasshouse?"

"Yes. It signifies that some of them interested her."

Beamish had a horrifying vision of some of the headlines that might more or less legitimately arise out of this exchange.

CID CONSIDERS SORCERERS' HELP—MURDERED WOMAN REFUSED ADMISSION TO WITCHES' SECRETS—PRESS PASS INFORMATION

TO POLICE—INSPECTOR SEES SIGNIFICANCE IN
GLASSHOUSE CONNECTION—

"Ladies and gentlemen," Mosley said. "You want my
help, and I want yours. I will meet you in the Crook Inn
at nine this evening, and I promise you a statement about
anything I consider you old enough to know."

Beamish noticed that Mosley signalled to the Social
Worker with an inclination of his head that might have been
no more than a loosening of his neck in his collar. Deirdre
Harrison slipped away from the edge of the crowd as Mosley
engaged their attention with a new cryptic point.

"There's just one thing I'd particularly ask you ladies
and gentlemen to do. And if you work with me, I think I
can promise every one of you a front-page by-line for the
next few mornings."

"What's that, then, Mr. Mosley?"

"Just keep well and truly out of my bloody sight," he
said.

Laughter: very thin, uncertain, and in most cases de-
layed. But by then Deirdre Harrison had made good her
escape.

Chapter Twelve

More than once Beamish had thought they were on the verge of calling on Priscilla Bladon at last. But each time, a fresh wave of reluctance seemed to strike the old man and he found some fresh excuse to postpone the confrontation. This time he looked up at the church clock, declared that the pub would be open but that at this hour even the most dedicated drinkers of Upper Marldale would still be at the substantial meal that they called tea.

And this turned out to be the case. There was one old chap who looked as if he never did go home, but was allowed to slumber alone in his corner during those hours when even the Crook could not avoid being closed. And there was one elderly gentleman, dapper in a shabbily genteel way, who, from the state of his glass, had just come in, dead-heating with the unbolting of the door. Mosley and this character—who responded to the rank of Major—appeared to be well acquainted with each other, though the Inspector declined to drink at the ex-soldier's expense. It was not long before Mosley had edged Major Hindle towards a shadowy corner and began putting low-key questions in a voice so diffident and quiet that Beamish, who was standing at his other elbow, had difficulty in picking up all the words.

"You'll forgive my asking—sir—routine, you know—question of elimination—what time did you leave this pub last night?"

The answer came with a touch of comic bluster.

"Didn't actually look at the clock, old man. Got to admit conversation sometimes carries us away. Wouldn't want to say anything to get the landlord into trouble."

Mosley countered this by not reacting at all. He simply waited until Hindle felt compelled to fill the silence.

"Bit after hours, got to admit. Still, I'm sure—"

"How long after hours? This could be important, Major."

"Sorry. Couldn't say within half an hour or so."

"A little after two, perhaps? I am asking others, too."

"God! Could it have been as late as that?"

"Where did you go, when you left here, Major?"

"Where did I go? Where do you think I'd go at two in the morning, man? I went home."

Hindle laughed: a brittle attempt at ridicule that would surely have convinced no one.

"You did not pay any calls on the way?"

"Calls on the way, Mosley—at that time of night?"

"You're saying no, sir?"

"Of course I'm bloody well saying no."

"In that case I ha-have to ask you, sir—"

Mosley's diffidence went as far as a slight stammer. He seemed to hate himself for having to put the question.

"I have to ask you, then, when you were last at the Old Tollhouse."

There was no doubt that the dart homed in. And Hindle was so unskilled a dissimulator that he lost his temper.

"What the hell are you insinuating now? What bloody gossip is this that you've been listening to? Even on the level of good taste, Mosley, this is monstrous. I don't know what your superiors will say, but I'll certainly see they hear of this."

Mosley's head was slightly bowed: it could have been with shame and an implied apology.

"I would have thought on the whole," he said, "that we'd rather not have my superiors going round Upper Marldale asking this sort of question. I mean, between ourselves, there exists a need to know. *I* need to know. But once I do know, if the facts are irrelevant, there's an end to the matter."

He was not able to take it up further with Hindle at the moment, because they were interrupted by the arrival of the uniformed motor-cyclist with the papers that Grimshaw had sent. This officer had had previous experience of looking for Mosley in the deep country, and had made a bee-line for the Crook.

"Excuse me."

Mosley went over to a table and opened the envelope.

"Excuse me," he said again. "I must make a phone-call to my superiors."

Detective-Superintendent Grimshaw sat in his bed-room slippers in his armchair, sipped a whisky-and-water and cast an appraising eye down his first interim short-list of land-deals.

There was one that stuck out like the telegraph poles on Crumble Ridge, which was the name of the tract of country concerned. What drew Grimshaw's attention was that he could see no reason why the County Council should have wanted to acquire this bleak and sterile moor in the first place—unless to speculate on its resale value if a link-road between two trans-Pennine motorways were ever to be driven across it. As it was, the County resold the land within two years of purchase, at a profit that could scarcely have covered the survey and legal costs of the original conveyancing. Yet the new owners, a financial holding company, must have made a bomb when the earth-shifters for the link-road did finally move in.

The next case was a ten-acre parcel where the County boundary ran down to the edge of Bradcaster City. These fields had been bought in the early 1950s for extensions to the adjoining county grammar school, now a sixth-form college. On the face of it, there seemed reasonable grounds for selling: the falling birth-rate and the enlargement of a neighbourhood comprehensive certainly gave the impression that the land was now surplus to the requirements of the Education Department. It was sold to a massive hyper-market, despite vociferous opposition from the Bradcaster Chamber of Commerce.

But this was ignoring the overall picture. The Education Committee had aspirations in other directions. At the same time as the hypermarket deal was going through, a sports and leisure complex was being envisaged for an

overspill estate not three quarters of a mile away. Fifteen
acres were needed for the establishment and its accompa-
nying playing-fields, but the populace had to be satisfied
in the end with half that area—bought at a quarter of a
million pounds more than the hypermarket had paid for
their freehold.

Finally, Grimshaw had been struck by a transaction on
a much more modest financial scale. Evenlode, an old people's home on one of the hills bordering Bradburn, had
been discontinued and the property put on the market: a
not extensive former country house in secluded grounds.
A strong case had been made out: general retrenchment
was required by central government. The property needed
much spent on it both structurally and from the sanitary
point of view. Its distance from town was highly inconven-
ient for the old people and their relatives. And more sheltered housing in the heart of Bradburn was promised within
ten years' time. What happened to the old people of Evenlode was not recorded in the minutes. Few of them could
have afforded the fees of the private nursing home which
bought the property. In no case did the minutes answer
the key questions. They contained a statement of final decisions, of facts, dates and figures. They did not recapitulate
the arguments, the infighting or the wheeler-dealing that
must have gone on in sub-committees, official and unofficial, before party whips finally dictated the block voting in
full Council. The common ground in all three cases was
that it was outsiders, and not the County rate-payers who
had benefited both financially and in the matter of amenities. Whether there were any common personalities among
these outsiders was the crux of the matter—that was the
missing link at which the DPP's assistant had jibbed. The
tangle of frontmen, nominees and holding companies was
something that Grimshaw knew he had not the expertise
to unravel. But he did know that there was common ground
on the local-government side. County Councillor Harry
Whitcombe had been the genial committee chairman in
every case. Grimshaw poured himself another whisky and
picked up the phone. He dialled his office to ask if there
were any operational messages that he ought to know about

before he went to bed. Having heard what there was, he dictated one short memo to be transmitted forthwith to Mosley.

Public bar at Crook Inn unsuitable as Incident Room. Find alternative at once. T.G., Det-Sup.

They were finally going to Priscilla Bladon's. On their way Beamish ventured to query Mosley's future policy towards Major Hindle.

"Oh, he'll come to us. He'll be so damned scared in case a word of this gets to his wife."

"You really think he was at the Tollhouse last night?"

"Damned sure he wasn't. Bed was slept in by two other people. Hairs from their privates prove that. Grimshaw has sent me the path notes."

"So what do you hope to gain from him?"

"Pillow talk."

And the thought seemed to bring Mosley genuine merriment.

"If you can imagine what Hindle and Mrs. Cater found to chat about between their passionate exertions."

"I must say I find the thought of that liaison both astonishing and more than slightly sickening."

"Do you? We never know what any of us might come to, Beamish."

"Really, Inspector—"

"Think I'm a dirty old man, do you? These things happen, laddie."

"I know that. But—"

"It boils down to physics in the long run, Beamish— the incompressibility of liquids. The relief of hydrostatic pressures becomes imperative on the one hand, and both parties enjoy an exchange of sensations—or at least, the never-dying hope of a sensation. Plus the fact that the two of them are working hard to convince themselves that they aren't past it."

"Yes. I understand all that. It's the final image that I find revolting."

"Not so revolting as the final image of the other couple in Mrs. Cater's bed."

"I must confess I haven't got the weight of them yet."

"I have. Professional killers."

"You're convinced of that, aren't you?"

"I see nothing else that fits the bill."

"All right. Hypothesis accepted. So why leap into bed? At the very moment when they ought to be putting miles behind them?"

"They're professional killers for two reasons. One's the contract fee. The other's the joy they get from the moment of performance: and by performance, I mean killing. Killing turns them on—I believe that's the favoured terminology. No bag over the victim's face, remember?"

A little man in a homburg—a homburg that he ought to have exchanged for a new one at least a couple of years ago; a little man in his mid-fifties who looked a good deal older; a little man in a navy-blue suit that shone at the knees, and whose jacket-pockets appeared to be stuffed with potatoes. His mind had no right to be running on lines like these.

"Don't think I'm pontificating, Beamish. How can you and I know? But something must go on in the minds of a pair of professional killers. They do a deliberate, Home Office job on Beatrice Cater. They watch her face death. And it turns them on. The bed's there."

"I still think—"

"Damn it, it wouldn't take them long, Beamish, worked up as they were. Don't you see, lad—"

The unwonted enthusiasm of a man who had just seen something else—

"Don't you see—that's why they moved the corpse? Maybe the lady's on the fussy side. Maybe she didn't care for a spot of how's-your-father with that thing hanging there. So they moved it into the next room, hung it from the beam. Wouldn't take a couple of minutes. And I'll bet the other thing didn't take a couple of minutes, either."

"But if you're right—and I'm not saying you are—this is all a long way from anything we know or can prove—doesn't this give us a *modus operandi?*"

"I've heard people sling terms like that about."

But Beamish's enthusiasm was turned on now.

"Just let's say you're right: a couple who can't resist coitus immediately after they've killed. Then that's their *modus operandi*, a felon's hallmark. They're getting these things computerized these days."

"Are they, by God?"

"At the CRO."

"Oh aye?"

"The Criminal Records Office."

Mosley looked as if it was news to him that there was any such institution.

"We ought to ask them for a search," Beamish said. "Just in case—"

Mosley looked unimpressed.

"Well, will you leave it to me, Mr. Mosley? Just as soon as we've finished with this witch, I'll get on to the Met—"

Mosley shrugged, as if he saw little point in it, but had no wish to spoil Beamish's fun.

"To tell you the truth," he said, "if they're contract killers, they don't interest me all that much. They'll be a long way from these parts by now, and as people they're probably deadly boring. The man I want my little chat with is the one who put them under contract."

"Well—that's what matters, of course—"

"It's all you and I can hope to achieve, laddie, stuck up here in this wilderness. Anyway, here we are—"

And Priscilla Bladon opened the front door to them as she saw them halfway up her drive. A big woman: in her eighties, they said—though she could have passed herself off as sixty-five. Beamish remembered to look at her hands—and understood what Mosley had meant about them.

Chapter Thirteen

Priscilla Bladon's house was a big one by Upper Marldale standards, built in the later Georgian years. Miss Bladon
led them through an expanse of entrance hall into an even
more spacious drawing-room with a handsome bow window
overlooking a large walled garden now beginning to sink
into first twilight.

The room needed to be spacious not to be over-
whelmed by all that was in it. It was incongruity on the
grand scale rather than actual disorder that set the tone.
African tribal masks kept company with warriors' shields
and drums. An exquisitely carved Polynesian paddle lay
athwart a Renaissance bass-viol. A fruit-bowl in Hindu brass
contained half a dozen immobilized hand-grenades. There
were urns, bowls and ewers in earthenware and porcelain,
as well as vessels fashioned from gourds from every latitude.
The empty shell of an armadillo lay upside down as a re-
ceptacle for thimbles, lace-makers' bobbins, wax fruit and
lumps of coral.

There was something abysmally depressing about the
collection, some over-riding influence that deadened the
room. Beamish decided that it emanated from the ubiquity
of stuffed animals, almost every one the craftsmanship of
the less sensitive breed of taxidermist. They ranged from
squirrels, parrots and a forest pig to a moronic wallaby who
had a boomerang between his teeth, as if, ironically, he had
just retrieved it. In her scholastic days, Miss Bladon had
made every class she taught "adopt" a merchant ship, which
led to voluminous correspondence—and a gift from every
home-coming master who made landfall within visiting distance of Marldale.

One effect of the melancholy miscellany was to dwarf

two of the three women who had been waiting here for the police to call. Priscilla Bladon was not dwarfed. In crossing the room to show the two men in she had, as it were, imprinted an enduring impression: she accommodated her physical size by exaggerating it, rather than by an attempt to draw the eye away—she was wearing a long, flowing dress that made very little contact with her body below the bust and its floral pattern was bold and colourful. She was sitting now on a chintzy armchair, was clearly not truly at her ease on any other chair in the room. Susan Bexwell was at the opposite side of the hearth, her long pony-tail drawing her hair tight across her scalp, her round, slim-rimmed spectacles seeming to proclaim her an honours mathematics graduate. Deirdre Harrison sat with her trousered legs curled up on a priceless strip of Kurdistan carpet, the straps of her bib-and-brace even more awry than when Beamish had last seen her.

Mosley came to the point.

"Well—who killed her?"

"Outsiders," Priscilla Bladon said, her voice a confident contralto.

"You sound sure."

"If it had been someone local, somebody would have known."

"So why kill her?"

"Because of what she knew."

"And what did she know?"

"That's what we couldn't find out."

"I thought she invited you three up there to tell you."

"She did. Subject to terms. Which we couldn't agree."

Slight pause; end of first phase of question and answer.

"Aren't you going to tell us her terms?" Mosley asked.

"No."

"You mean that you three still mean to go it alone?"

"We stand a better chance than you do."

"Only by withholding information," Mosley said.

"Have we withheld information in the past? Our difficulty has been getting information listened to."

"You haven't had the sort of information that people are prepared to listen to. You don't *know* what someone wants

with Ned Suddaby's field. You don't know *why* Herbert
Garside wants to keep people off his footpath. Now, I suppose the implication is that Beatrice Cater had found out."

"She thought she had."

"She must have come pretty close to the mark," Mosley
said, "for them to have killed her for it. What price they'll
try to kill you next?"

"That lightning daren't strike here again."

"A very dangerous assumption, Miss Bladon."

End of second phase.

"So," Mosley went on. "You're going it alone. Only
you can't. Because you won't be alone. I'm on the road too."

"We're not in competition, Mr. Mosley. We just want
to make sure somebody gets there."

"Which means more conjuring tricks, I suppose?"

"Conjuring tricks, Mr. Mosley? You should be more
respectful."

"Well, what were they but conjuring tricks? Putting
dud eggs under some poor smallholder's broody. And obviously you sent someone up the old church tower, whilst
you diverted attention with your *Danse Macabre* round the
gravestones."

"Wally Brewer, from Chapel Burton. He does their
clock."

"It's obvious what sort of contribution Flavour Control,
Ltd. made to local unfeline behaviour. And while we're on
the subject, I must warn you—watch what you're doing
with toxic substances at Hadley Dale Dog Trials."

"We will, Mr. Mosley."

"I must admit that you have our police laboratories
puzzled over those withered cabbages."

"We whipped the good ones out and planted dead ones."

"Very commendable social behaviour, that, I'm sure.
And I'm still perplexed by the winning darts throw."

Miss Bladon nodded gravely.

"That was touch and go—the only real risk we've taken
up to now. That was the only stunt that rose above the
strictly materialistic plane. But Harry Akeroyd's a very good
darts-player—and also very highly suggestible. I should
know: I taught him from the ages of five to fourteen. I taught
him all he knows—bar playing darts. I took a chance, I'll

admit. I put it firmly into his mind what he was going to do. He believed it—and he did it."

"Thank God!" Deirdre Harrison said.

Mosley brought Beamish into the conversation for the first time since they had come in.

"My friend and colleague here is an unsophisticated man by Upper Marldale standards. I don't think he has fully grasped yet why you've had to turn to magic."

Priscilla Bladon turned patiently to Beamish. He expected her to have a slightly amused contempt for him, if not the superior conviction that he could be ignored altogether. At the best he expected to be patronized, but on the contrary she treated him with the same sort of respect she might have given to a child who wanted the answer to an intelligent question.

"Because it's a waste of time talking sense to people," she said, and waited to see if this sank in. "People don't believe in magic, but wouldn't they just love to? Given the opportunity, they'll even pretend to. They *loved* that business with the church clock, even though every man jack of them knew it must be a fiddle. But if we'd tried to persuade them to bring Wally Brewer in to wind it up, they'd have gone on arguing for weeks. Somebody would have heard that Wally was no good. Somebody else wouldn't have wanted to bring talent in from Chapel Burton. Somebody would have known a better man. Somebody would have argued about how much to pay him, and what fund it was going to come out of. Somebody would have asked if we'd got him insured while he was up the tower. I've always been one for getting on with things."

Once she got into full spate, it was difficult to interrupt Priscilla Bladon.

"Look at television advertising. It must work, or they wouldn't spend on it what they do. But do they talk sense? If they want you to give yourself lung cancer with a new brand of cigarette, they show you a girl standing by a waterfall. Does anybody think there's any connection? No: but they smoke the cigarettes. If they want you to buy a petrol of the same chemical composition as anybody else's petrol, they show you a tiger prancing along a sea-shore. Have they listened to me when I've tried to warn them about Suddaby's field and Garside's footpath? No: when I tried to present a reasoned case at the parish meeting a sigh went round the room—that daft old woman's on her feet again. But when I dance to a gramophone round the Mawdesley vault, they start paying attention."

"But what do you want them to do with Suddaby's field?" Beamish asked her.

"We want a recreation ground for our children," Susan Bexwell said.

"Or something for somebody. The point is, that field is a public asset. It belongs to Upper Marldale. A few square inches of it belongs to me, because I was a ratepayer when the Council bought it. Then we suddenly hear it's on the market, with what they call outline planning permission—which shows that somebody in some Council office has been scheming it out for months. Is it going to make an atom of difference to next year's rates, the price they'll get for Ned Suddaby's? No—any transaction that involves public property in this county is done for one reason only—because somebody stands to gain from it."

"And we do want a playing-field."

Mrs. Bexwell must have said her piece on every available platform in Marldale.

"They've got the notion in Bradburn and Pringle that country children don't need amenities. If a child lives in the country, his life's made—that's what people think. Well: take a walk round Upper Marldale any evening: not even a street-lamp to sit on the kerb under. A child in the country has nothing—but *nothing*."

"So somebody on the back row of the meeting tells her she doesn't have to live here."

"And it isn't only Marldale," Deirdre Harrison said. "It's going on all over the country. What happened to the Evenlode Home up Bradburn Brow? What about the hypermarket on the Bradcaster by-pass? What about the new sports centre? And what name comes to mind whenever you see a theodolite being lifted out of a county van? Harry Whitcombe."

"It's all right talking like that within these four walls," Mosley warned her. "Don't forget you're a public employee."

"That's why we feel we need a touch of witchcraft here and there, Mr. Beamish."

At that point the door-bell rang—one of those simple wire-pulled mechanisms that set up a jangle in the hall. Priscilla Bladon got up and swept out of the room with a flourish of her dress that endangered a rich variety of relics.

"Of course, we do realize that there could be other ways of setting about this," Susan Bexwell said. "But it's been—well—amusing, until now."

"It looked as if it was going to work, too," Deirdre Harrison added.

"Past tense?" Mosley asked her. "You mean that what's happened to Beatrice Cater is giving you furious second thoughts?"

"Public opinion in Marldale is not going to care for monkeying about for some time to come."

"You've put that to Miss Bladon?"

"She's got some idea of her own. I wish I knew what it was."

"Did Mrs. Cater want to be associated with your witchery?"

"Far from it. She regarded it as in bad taste, pointless and in some vague way, I think, blasphemous. No sense of humour, of course. A silly woman, in fact, though she would stick at things once she got an idea into her head."

"Obviously she was working on this alleged corruption from some angle of her own. Have you any idea what the angle was?"

"Not for sure. She made a number of trips into Bradburn. Major Hindle ran her up in his car."

"Hadn't she a car of her own?"

"Off the road. And what with one thing and another, Hindle was hardly in a position to refuse. We think she was cultivating someone in County Hall."

"But no idea who?"

"Priscilla's been working on it."

Then they pricked up their ears at the sound of voices in the hall. It sounded like an invasion in force: the media. Beamish wondered how Mosley would manage to get rid of them.

Chapter Fourteen

Beamish counted twenty-five of them, but thought he could have missed someone in the confusion. There were cub reporters who looked eager, youngsters who looked conceited, others cynical and some bored. There were old professionals, hard-bitten, with nicotine-stained fingers. There were young women in jeans and one in a patchwork caftan. There were Minoltas, Ricohs, Olympuses, Pentaxes and a prominent Hasselblad. Even the most blasé was momentarily knocked back by the impact of the extraordinary room. Flashes were busy all over the place and it seemed as if everything and everybody was being photographed at once. One woman had hold of the South Sea Island paddle and another was plucking a string of the bass-viol.

"Do, please, handle anything you want to. I always used to feel with children in school that it was frustration only to see things in glass cases."

There was no irony in this at all. Miss Bladon seemed far from put out by the onslaught, appeared indeed to welcome the chaos.

"We'd half expected to find you sitting round a cauldron."

"Cauldrons are out," she said. "We do our newts' eyes in a micro-wave oven nowadays."

"Would you like to make a prediction, Miss Bladon? About the Tollhouse murderer?"

"We understand that Mrs. Cater was not a member of your coven. Is it true that you'd turned her down?"

"Would you and your friends accept a challenge from the *Morning Herald*, Miss Bladon?"

"Would it be true to say that you have been prophesying that something like this was going to happen, Miss Bladon?"

"It certainly would not," she said.

"We understand that your next coup is to be at a Sheep Dog Trial, Miss Bladon. Would you care to enlarge on that?"

"What is the connection between the late Mrs. Cater and a footpath across a farmer's field?"

"How does the field called Ned Suddaby's fit into the picture?"

It was not to be doubted that the invaders had already discovered the resident oracles of the Crook.

"When is the next plenary session of your coven?"

Miss Bladon went to a shallow drawer in a Chinese lacquered cabinet and brought out a football referee's whistle, which she blew within a couple of inches of Beamish's ear.

"Ladies and gentlemen—I almost said *children*—"

The silence that she produced was so galvanic that it might indeed have been wrought by the casting of a spell.

"If you will find seats for yourselves—please do not hesitate to lower your posteriors on to any article of furniture that looks capable of bearing your weight—I will endeavour to answer your questions. But I warn you in advance that I will turn a deaf ear to anything I consider silly and that I rapidly become bored if required to repeat the obvious. Moreover, nobody else's mouth will be open at any time that mine is and anyone wishing to say anything will first put up his hand in the normal civilized way. I will then invite him to speak unless I have taken exception to something he has already said. Now—sort yourselves out."

Stools, corners of sofas and vacant floor spaces were sought and occupied and twenty-five journalistic hands were raised high above heads.

"Ladies first—"

She pointed to a young woman with enormous spectacles.

"How seriously do you expect us to take your reputation for sorcery, Miss Bladon?"

"I think it would be prudent to play safe with it, ma'am."

"In other words, you are serious about it?"

"Do I look a flippant type?"

"Do you mean that you are dabbling in diabolism?"

"Not at all. Nothing so foul."

"But alliance with the devil was surely the basis of medieval witchcraft?"

"If you will read your social history more carefully, you might conclude that the ritual was a cover for an early feminist movement."

"So that is what you and your friends are trying to achieve in Marldale? You are an ardent feminist?"

"I am seldom criticized for being submissive to males. Or to females either, for that matter."

"It does seem to me, Miss Bladon, that your so-called feats in this village could have all been contrived by artificial means."

"You are welcome to try to contrive them by any means you can think of. What paper are you?"

"The *Guardian*."

"What a pity you didn't come to my school. I'd have taught you to spell. You, sir—"

She pointed to a man whose hand was signalling more vigorously than the rest.

"Davies of the *Courier*. I wouldn't like us to get bogged down in this sideline, Miss Bladon. It *is* only a sideline, and some of us do cater for a readership that prefers facts to sensations. What we are here for is a death that the police are treating as murder—the death of an interesting woman."

"I am glad to have you remind us of that, sir."

"A sculptress, I believe?"

"I really do think she believed that herself. Not that any of us are aware that she had ever done any sculpture, but I am quite sure that she hoped to, one day. That would be sufficient for her to confer the title upon herself."

"You are suggesting that she went about deceiving people?"

"Never until after she had succeeded in deceiving herself. You might say that that entails a kind of honesty. Between ourselves we used to call her the Great Pretender."

They heard an unplaceable whisper of *nil nisi bonum*.

"You are failing to understand. We used the term kindly.

We knew what she had to contend with. After all, she had been Trixie Lowther."

"Trixie Lowther?"

"Ah! Most of you are too young to remember. And some of you others may not have paid much attention at the time. The full mouthful was Lowther, Cross and Dickson, but there were only Lowthers left on the board by the time Trixie was getting mentioned now and then in the society columns."

"Lowther, Cross and Dickson—?"

"Brewers," Priscilla Bladon said. "Lowther's Blacksmith Bitter, Horseshoe IPA and Smithy Brown. Long since merged with the big boys, but there was a time when you saw the forge under the village chestnut on every edge-of-town hoarding. I can't tell you much about what life was like for Trixie Lowther when she was a girl. But from what little talk I ever had with her on the subject, it's clear that she was both spoiled and hemmed in. She was spoiled because not only must the Lowthers want for nothing— they must be seen to want for nothing. And she was shackled because there were certain values that were only questioned by the demented or the anti-social. I hope I'm not boring you? I promise you I'm coming to the point."

There were some murmurs of encouragement.

"Beatrice Lowther was neither demented nor anti-social. She was mentally alert without being clever. She didn't know enough about society to be on fire for reform. She'd never rubbed shoulders close enough with real life to believe that anything could threaten her survival. She did embrace unfashionable causes, but it was not because she knew anything beneath the surface of them. It was because they were different, because she was bored to tears of having to toe mindless social lines. She had a little surplus energy, a little surplus curiosity—and a lifelong deficit of judgement. Judgement can only be a series of comparisons with the yardsticks of your own experience. And if your experience amounts to nothing, what yardsticks can you have?"

"What causes did she embrace?" somebody asked.

"The Fascist dictators, with a preference for Nazi Germany. But that was largely coincidental. Beatrice Lowther was holidaying in Vienna with a girl-friend, a pair of eigh-teen-year-olds, in 1934. An attractive, inexperienced, harmlessly scatter-brained couple. Does the year 1934 mean anything to the present company?"

She looked round to their face for an answer—the routine of the classroom.

"No? The assassination of Dollfuss, the Austrian Chan-cellor. Actually, our all-but-bright young things had just started for home when the news broke and it was one of those railway journeys that we sometimes used to see in the thirties' cinema: long halts at benighted stations, lug-gage searched on freezing platforms, interminable and poker-faced identity checks. But somewhere between the Hohe Tauern and the Bavarian Alps the two English girls were rescued."

Was this how she used to tell *The Three Bears* to her assembled infants at the end of a drowsy afternoon?

"There was a party of strapping young Aryans a couple of compartments down the corridor, and no doubt there'd been a certain amount of eye-to-eye flirtation, exchanging frustrations when they couldn't get anything to eat or drink in a shut-down restaurant car. Somewhere between the frontier and Munich—one of those nowhere places—the train pulled up again, even the engine was shunted off. Beatrice and her friend and two of these Germans were at a corridor window, trying to see what was happening, when one of the men said, "Oh, to hell with this! Where are we? Not all that far from Rosenheim? I think I know how to improve on this as a means of transport. Would you two ladies care for a change of scenery?"

"So they got off at this god-forsaken village, and the men were apparently members of some political para-military in mufti, and carried papers that had people heiling Hitler. They had no difficulty hiring a car, but they didn't go any farther than some mountain guest-house for the night, and in view of the youth of some of my audience, I suppose we'd better draw a veil over anything else that might have happened."

She half rose, resettled her limbs in her chair.

"I'm sorry if I seem to be going on. I'm trying to get you to understand Beatrice Lowther-Cater. This affair does concern her, after all."

"How do you know all this?" the man from the *Courier* asked her.

"I've gone into it."

"From her own lips?"

"Not a lot of it from her own lips. I can't pretend that we were close."

There was a subtle change in Priscilla Bladon's tone. This was a point on which she did not want to be pressed. There was a slight ripple of restlessness among some of the reporters.

"She went back to Germany again the next year and the year after: the Rhine Valley, the Harz Mountains, the Black Forest—the usual. And clearly chance had given her the key to a certain stratum of the up-and-coming young leadership. You might find it difficult to understand how she could be taken in by them. I don't. Politically she was infantile. Impressionable she has always been. But they were exploiting a romanticism to which even some Anglo-Saxons were not immune: folk-guitars round pinewood camp-fires, Siegfried, Student Princes. And there were ambitious young Germans who felt they were reinforcing their own main chance by cultivating a sympathetic young lady from a supposedly influential family in the other camp. She had a much-publicized interview with a *Gauleiter*. And then, lo and behold, came an invitation to Berchtesgaden."

Miss Bladon made a combination of gesture and facial disclaimer that would have done credit to a French higher *bourgeoise*.

"I'm not saying that Hitler gave her much of his time, or that he was impressed, or that he thought he was achieving anything by seeing her. Slightly amused, perhaps, bored more likely—and given another fillip to his hopes that he could walk right over us when the time came. But she came home besotted, full of it, as near to an activist as she ever was in her lifetime: the injustice of Versailles, the loss of the African colonies, the impracticability of the Polish Corridor—that's how she talked to Territorial Army officers

at country-house dances in 1938. Those were the views she
bored her father's friends with. She joined the Link—a
suspect organization, that was banned the moment war did
break out. She took to writing voluminous letters to Germany in which, the rumour went, she was listing by-roads,
culverts and transformer-stations for the information of
forthcoming Panzer commanders.

"The Lowthers had her put away—quietly, respecta-
bly. There was a liberal-minded experiment, caring for the
mentally deranged in Eastern Belgium—at Gheel, in Prov-
ince Limburg. Patients from all over Europe were insti-
tutionally managed in large numbers, and wherever possible
were farmed out to civilian billets in a remote countryside.
That's how her family "lost" Trixie Lowther early in 1939.
And that's how she passed behind the German lines when
Belgium was overrun in 1940."

Miss Bladon was obviously not in command of all the
detail of the later stages of the story. She was beginning to
race and perhaps to skip some of what she did know. Trixie's
fees at Gheel were scrupulously paid via the Swiss Red
Cross throughout the war. There was no record of any attempt to pull strings and get her repatriated: she was an
embarrassment successfully put out of mind. Nor was there
any innuendo that the Germans, for the first few war years
at any rate, treated her other than correctly. As long as
people in her kind of predicament remained up against the
Wehrmacht or the older generation of administrator, it
was remarkable how often they did escape without major
maltreatment. In the later stages she was transferred to
internment, which was not without its greyness and priva-
tion—but millions fared worse.

And Beatrice Lowther's phenomenal ill-judgement let
her down again. She was one of a handful of stranded Britons
who accepted a few trivial privileges in exchange for making
radio broadcasts over the propaganda network. What she
had to say was pitifully harmless—and politically empty. It
amounted to no more than the sort of messages that might
have been passed with the dedication of a record request
on a Sunday-morning programme at home. But those who
drew up the official come-uppance lists saw things differ-

ently. There were others whose broadcasts had been reck-lessly damaging. Beatrice Lowther had to be classified with them, for had she not formally furnished succour and com-fort to the King's Enemies?

Consequently, her liberation in the late spring of 1945 was followed by her almost immediate arrest by the British, and then there were a few months of confinement, no less grey, though better catered for, than her internment by the Germans. Clearly mere brewers were not powerful enough to engineer her immediate release, but when it came to having cigarettes, novels, periodicals, a radio and even a sewing-machine delivered to her cell, it seemed she only had to ask. And then, one unexpected morning, she was taken before the Camp Commandant and told that no action was going to be taken against her.

Freedom was something to which she could not adjust herself at first. She wavered before decision of any kind. The CO assumed that she would be ecstatic at the prospect of being flown to the UK from the nearest military airstrip that same afternoon. But if there was one thing about which she was determined, it was that she was not returning to the Lowther fold, not ever. What she wanted was to go somewhere quiet, and spacious, and empty—where she could go for a country walk, hear a bird sing—and cry. She told the Commandant she wanted to go back to Gheel. There were villagers there who had been good to her. She had possessions there, which somebody might still be look-ing after for her. The Commandant looked at her as if he were beginning to believe that there must have been good grounds for sending her to Gheel in the first place. His sphere of experience did not tell him what facilities existed for a British civilian to travel independently to Belgium. He sent her over to the offices of the Control Commission.

And that was where she fell in love—not for the first time in her life, but this time leading to marriage not long after the first encounter. She was now thirty and her boy-friend was an established British civil servant called Ca-ter—a messenger, an opener of doors, a deliverer of files, and a pilot along corridors. When he found her, dazed and lost in one of the more bewildering of his corridors, Cater was courteous and kind to her. Throughout their life together, Cater was never anything but courteous and kind to her. He set her on a pedestal that elevated her far out of his own world. Cater was one of those who gained satisfaction from being of service—a handy quality in a civil service messenger. And when service transfers sent him to deliver files and open doors in Prague and Budapest, Beatrice moved with him within observing distance of the *corps diplomatique*.

Cater had died ten years ago. Four years ago she had come to Upper Marldale to set up her establishment as a sculptress.

"And you are suggesting," the man from the *Courier* asked, "that what has happened to Mrs. Cater has its roots in something thirty-odd years old?"

"I am not suggesting anything. It is not my role to come to conclusions. I am not an investigator. Our investigator has been very patient with me for the last half-hour."

She extended an arm in a leg-of-mutton sleeve to present Mosley with the floor.

"Ladies and gentlemen," Mosley said. "I have an appointment for a press conference with you all in the Crook at nine o'clock. It is already half past. I apologize."

"They won't be closed yet," someone muttered.

"Indeed they won't. In fact I sometimes wonder if the Crook is not trying to beat the record of the London Windmill Theatre. But will it suffice for now if I just tell you that I am in possession of a vital clue, and that I hope to make an interesting announcement in the not-too-distant future?"

He hung behind the exodus of journalists to speak to Beamish.

"Beamish, go down at once to Lower Marldale and do one of your training-course searches on the bedroom that the punks occupied on the night Mrs. Cater was killed."

"Sir."

Beamish did a half-turn on his heel, then half-turned back.

"Am I looking for anything in particular, sir?"

"I'd hate to prejudice you by putting ideas into your head, Sergeant. Though I'd prefer to hope that they're there already."

"Sir?"

"Look for any evidence that the punks weren't punks. And that two of them didn't spend the night there."

Then Mosley hurried after the column of the press and fetched up alongside the young woman from the *Guardian*.

"I take it that you're going to the Crook, miss?"

"Do you know of anywhere else to go?"

"When you get there, look for a retired Major. I don't think you'll miss him. Sort of fire-eater who was probably a glorified storeman two hundred and fifty miles behind the line."

"I think I've noticed him already."

"Tell him that I've slipped up to his cottage to have a chat with his wife."

Chapter Fifteen

Despite the absence of street lighting, it was possible to diagnose a good deal of the late-evening activity of Upper Marldale. Irregular triangles of curtain-filtered light fell across the uneven pavements and here and there a socially minded villager, perhaps expecting a visitor, had provided an electric bulb over his door, so that the facia of the Craft Shop was legible and even the front elevation of the Community Centre could be made out by those who already knew it was there. The hospitable inn sign of the Crook cast its invitation generously beyond its own forecourt, but by far the most prolific source of illumination during the half-hour after the meeting in Miss Bladon's house was the procession of journalists' headlamps. Many had now given up hope of using the phones in the Market Square and the pub and were driving off to seek communication from other villages; or in some cases were heading direct to their offices in Manchester, South Yorkshire or the West Riding.

Beamish was aware of peace and darkness settling over him as he drove down the Marl Valley for the second time that day. Here and there the windows of a farmhouse showed up wanly on some improbable flankside site, but for miles at a stretch there was no manifestation of life whatsoever as he edged cautiously round the hairpins. And then he became aware that there were tail-lamps ahead of him, pinpoints of red that rose and fell with the vagaries of the mad road.

Whoever it was in front was driving at a speed that Beamish would not have risked. At one stage the other vehicle got so far ahead that it seemed to have disappeared supernaturally into the night, but a mile later he had a momentary glimpse of its spots of red light as they vanished yet again round the corner of a falling bank. He had lost sight of it once more by the time he had reached Lower Marldale, and was unable to pick out any car, inside or outside the Old Glasshouse compound, that could have been the one he had been following.

Joe Murray: that was the name that Deirdre Harrison had quoted as the one-man reception committee for the punks. Beamish found Joe Murray—and he was the one from whom Mosley had been on the verge of buying a present for his niece. Joe was still at work at one of his benches, turning the stem of what looked to be a standard lamp.

"I've been waiting for you to show up again."

Beamish told him what he wanted to see, and Murray conducted him past several huts. But when he came to the annexe that he wanted, the craftsman held up his arm to restrain the sergeant.

"There's somebody in there."

And there was—a torchlight, darting back and forth behind the crudely curtained windows. So Beamish had to go through the melodrama of an approach from cover, and when he finally thrust open the door, he was prepared for anything. Almost anything, that is, except what he actually found: the person on hands and knees in a corner of the cubicle, examining a few loose papers that were strewn there, was Deirdre Harrison.

Chapter Sixteen

It was impossible to look at Mrs. Hindle without wondering how she and the Major could have met, courted and settled down into a married life which each had learned to tolerate. Perhaps her drop-shots at the net had been the perfect complement to his service: though she hardly looked as if she had ever been a Joan Hunter Dunne. And there was little doubt that one of the most salutary features in their union must have been Hindle's long absences overseas. One wondered what they could possibly ever have found to talk about. Was she a prop and support to him in his fashioning of walking-sticks? And was he prostrate with admiration for the economy and taste with which she maintained her ragbag?

It was the contents of this ragbag that she had out on the table when Mosley called, and she seemed to think that this in itself provided grounds for shame. She began stuffing bits of material back, spilling some on chairs and on the floor, utterly undoing any sorting out that she had had in progress.

"It's the Major, you see. He does so dislike my having any work in sight about the house after what he calls *Retreat*."

A very nervous woman.

"I'm sorry that the Major's out. He does so like a glass of beer just now and then. And I think it's good for a man to meet other men sometimes, don't you, Inspector?"

"Oh, I dare say you can tell me all I need to know," Mosley said.

The thought clearly horrified her. To be asked questions! To have to give specific answers—answers with which the Major was bound to disagree when she felt bound to tell him of them afterwards!

"I don't really think there's anything about this dreadful business that I can possibly tell you," she said.

"I'm just trying to pick up a few impressions of the late Mrs. Cater."

"Well, I don't see how I can help you in that respect at all. We hardly knew the poor woman."

"But you must have met her. I would have thought, in a community as small as this you'd have come across her now and then: church, charity functions, coffee mornings—"

"We have our friends, Inspector, and Mrs. Cater had hers—"

"And never the twain shall meet?"

"Mr. Mosley—the last thing on earth which I would wish to appear would be a snob."

"I'm quite sure that you're not, Mrs. Hindle."

"Mrs. Cater was so close to these dreadful people down in Lower Marldale—people on social security—"

"That does not necessarily make them criminals, you know."

"Oh, dear—have I put my foot in it again? Oh, I do wish William was here."

Perhaps a life of saying wrong things had left her with the conviction that William was always right. Maybe during their early life in married quarters she had learned by catastrophe to trust his authority on matters of precedence and protocol.

"I wouldn't expect your husband's views about Mrs. Cater to be greatly different from your own," Mosley said.

He heard the key of the latch and the opening of the front door, he heard the sounds of Hindle rapidly changing his shoes for slippers in the hall. So the *Guardian* reporter had done as he asked and told the Major that he had come here. So the Major must have finished his current drink in record time and left the Crook at a record early hour. Mosley raised his voice so that it carried to the hall.

"I would hardly expect your husband to know Mrs. Cater better than you do, Mrs. Hindle."

At which instant the Major came noisily into the room.

For a moment it looked as if he was going to lose his temper, demand a reason for the intrusion, postulate outraged citizen's rights, refuse to treat with anyone lower than the Chief. But he caught Mosley's eye, and Mosley was looking at him with the self-satisfaction of a man who knew where he had been spending some of his nights. Major Hindle disciplined himself. And as an embarrassed cat will wash himself, Major Hindle's customary withdrawal from an undesired engagement was into jocularity: a forced, false and unimpressive jocularity that he had not the wit to nourish.

"Hullo, hullo, hullo—got a warrant to arrest dear Hilda, have you?"

Mosley smiled at him broadly, as if he were the one man on the globe that he was glad to see again.

"Hardly. Just adding to my impressionistic knowledge of the late Mrs. Cater."

"Well, I don't think Hilda will be able to help you much. Not kindred souls at all—thank God!"

"I was just asking Mrs. Hindle whether she thought you knew Beatrice Cater better than she did."

"Well—I must say that's an odd point of view. What a curious thing to ask a man's wife."

"Is it true, do you think?"

"Why on earth should you think that?"

"Well, it could be the case, now, couldn't it?"

Hindle stared into Mosley's face as if to challenge him. But an actual verbal challenge was something to which he dared not rise.

"Well, it certainly isn't the case, Inspector," he said, in a crisp tone fully worthy of an officer of field rank.

"But you agree, in theory, that it could be the case?" What had got into Mosley that he kept chewing at this, like a terrier at a rat already dead?

"Really, Mosley, I don't know what you're getting at."

And Hindle paused, white-faced, wishing he had not said that. It could be the trigger that would have Mosley spilling the beans: he might be only too ready to say what he was getting at.

"Just asking around, sir, that's all, really," Mosley said aimlessly—then came back insidiously into the danger area.

"People talk so, in a village."

"Oh, God—I know that. And I should think in your job you know how little attention to pay to gossip—"

Then at last he grasped the nettle.

"I've had enough of your innuendo, Inspector Mosley. I demand to know: who has been talking about me, and what have they been saying?"

"Oh—I'm sure it amounts to nothing, Major."

Hindle looked at him blank-faced, and then suddenly laughed—a dry, staccato and mirthless laugh. "I suppose it's because twice in the last month I ran Mrs. Cater to Bradburn in my car."

He turned to put that matter right with his wife.

"I think I probably forgot to mention it to you, darling. Her car was off the road. It was going to take two or three weeks to get it fit to pass its MoT test. She had calls she wanted to make. Mostly at council offices, I think—you know how many irons she always had in how many fires—"

Mrs. Hindle seemed to have no difficulty in accepting the explanation. But she was looking worried, making twisting movements with her fingers. Perhaps she was fretful about the scene that must follow because she had been caught with her ragbag out after hours.

"That's the only thing I can think of," Hindle said.

"I don't suppose you remember which council offices?"

"I don't think I ever knew. Oh, she may have *said*. The woman never stopped talking there and back. One has to develop a defence mechanism. One switches off. One simply learns how not to listen."

"But I'm sure you have a general idea of what it was all about."

"I don't see that it matters."

"Everything might possibly matter. I've learned the hard way that in cases like this, Major Hindle, everything is information."

"She had some ploy on about a footpath and a field. God!—there must have been people in County Hall who fled at her approach."

During this interchange, Mrs. Hindle was making vigorous efforts to attract her husband's attention. He must have known this, but obstinately avoided looking her way. Mosley came to her rescue.

"Did you want to say something, Mrs. Hindle?"

"Oh—I don't think I ought to put my oar in—really—"

In front of a stranger, Hindle had to be courteous to her.

"No, darling—if there's something that you think might be helpful—"

"No. It was nothing."

"I think it was something," Mosley said, with a firmness that he usually seemed to keep in reserve, and that was difficult to withstand when he did bring it out. Mrs. Hindle found it impossible to withstand. Now there were tears in her eyes.

"What is it, darling?"

"Oh, William—I do wish—"

"What do you wish, darling?"

"Oh, I know I'm speaking out of turn. But I do wish you'd tell Inspector Mosley everything. It's bound to come out sooner or later."

"I'm sure everything's going to come out sooner or later. But neither Inspector Mosley nor I has the foggiest idea what you are talking about, my dear."

"I mean the camp, William."

"The camp?"

"In Germany."

"Oh, that—"

Hindle produced his jolly laugh again.

"How one's wife does love to protect one. Didn't mention this to you, Mosley—didn't want to complicate matters at this stage with irrelevancies from the past. Would have got round to telling you before long. You see, I met Mrs. Cater years ago. End of the war. I was Commanding Officer of a transit camp for civilian internees: sort of job they gave a man when his battalion broke up. Mrs. Cater—Trixie Lowther as she was in those days—was one of my clients. Not that I had much to do with her: routine administration, until one day I had the pleasure of informing her that they were not going to proceed against her. Sheer coincidence that she turned up in Marldale. You could have knocked me down with the proverbial thingummy."

Chapter Seventeen

"Bugger it!"

Deirdre Harrison unbent from her examination of grubby papers on the floor.

"Just my sodding luck!"

"What are you doing here?" Sergeant Beamish asked her.

"Same as you are. Trying to find out who spent the bloody night here."

"Except that I'm entitled to be here, and you're going to have to do some very fast talking in the next minute or two."

"Oh, Christ!" she said. "I would have to run into your bloody type."

"Keep on talking, Miss Harrison. I'll give you two minutes to come up with something credible."

"I just wanted to know who spent the night here."

"You know someone who might have done, I take it?"

"Bloody dozens of 'em. And there are one or two I'd be very sorry to see cadging a lift on this sort of shit-cart."

"Names? Whereabouts? Reasons for suspicion?"

"Oh, for the love of O'Riley, Sergeant. That would only be starting up hares. Absolute waste of your time. Don't you see, I just want to *eliminate*?"

"Eliminate for me, too, then."

"I'm buggered if I will."

He held out his hand.

"Give me your car keys. Wait for me outside."

"Have a heart, Sergeant. It's bloody draughty out there."

"Do as I say."

"And do you think I couldn't lose you in this camp? Get that door between us, and you'll have Marldale to search for me. Better keep me where you've got your eyes on me. I know you don't want me to see how you go to work. But do you think that you and I are on different sides? Look—I'll go and stand in that far corner with my face to the wall like a naughty bloody kid, if that'll make you feel more comfortable. And then when you've finished, I'd like to come with you to see Jack Mosley."

She went into the corner furthest from the door, a gross, shambling, round-shouldered, ill-dressed wench. But she had not been in position more than a few seconds before she turned her spotty face back over her shoulder.

"I'm sorry, Sergeant. I just couldn't wait. I never can. If you did my job and lived my life, one lesson you'd soon learn would be to get on with things yourself."

Beamish ignored her, turned to sift through the papers that she had been examining. There seemed very little that could tell him anything: sheets of old newspaper, the guarantee card for a transistor radio, a few old envelopes.

He spoke across to her.

"Who is A. W. Canniff? Know him?"

"He spent a month here. At present the guest of Her Majesty—misrepresentation for family allowance purposes."

"Charming friends you have."

"Bollocks!" she said.

"I'm sorry. That wasn't fair. You might as well blame me for screwsmen and Paki-bashers."

"I do."

"How do you work that out?"

"You're supposed to see them put away, aren't you?"

"Bollocks to you too, then."

He gave his general attention to the room: a stained and slashed poster that had once been a map of French vineyards; another, more recent, of the Who; two double-tier bunks, to neither of which he would care to trust his weight; one threadbare blanket, so filthy that no one this side of despair would want it near his body.

It was possible, in theory—sometimes—to look at a room and read the signs of things that had happened in it. Beamish looked round this one and was unable to think of anything except his disgust at the thought of anyone shutting himself in here without scrubbing the place out and

fumigating it first. What were the two questions that Mosley
had sent him here to answer? Were they real punks, and
how many of them had spent the night here? He examined
each of the bunks in turn, decided that it was touch and go
whether any of them was serviceable. But he could see
nothing to suggest whether any of them had been occupied
or not.

Deirdre Harrison was now openly looking back over
her shoulder again.

"Trying to sus out how many actually did overnight
here, Sergeant?"

"Have you sussed it out?"

"One," she said.

"What makes you so certain?"

"Can I come out of my corner?"

"For half a minute."

She loped across the room, went towards the wall under the vineyard poster.

"Space the area of one sleeping-bag has been swept
out here. Not with a broom, because there isn't one. With
an old newspaper or something. Fastidious bugger, obviously."

"You could be right."

"Of course I'm right. And I'm not trying to be clever.
I'm not trying to take the piss, Sergeant. You'd have spotted
it. I've been in here longer than you have."

"All right. Back to your corner. No—you can stay
out—if you'll tell me anything else you think you've worked
out."

"Well, there is one thing. Aren't they supposed to have
had three-cornered sex in here?"

"How do you know that?" he snapped at her, his suspicions alerted again.

"Joe Murray told me. He's the one who reported it to
Mosley. Have you ever had three-cornered sex, Sergeant?"

"Have you?"

"I was educated in a big school. But wouldn't you say,
Sergeant Beamish, speaking from your ivory tower of cold
chastity, that a threesome requires space? And must make
some impact on the environment?"

They both looked round the room again. The area where

the sleeping-bag had lain was the only space where the dust and litter had been disturbed for months.

"So—given that Joe Murray is no sensationalist, and knows the meaning of what he heard—"

"A tape-recorder," Beamish said, and his eye travelled at once to the power-point in the room.

"Actually, I'm surprised that the power's still on," he said.

"Are you? Why? It's the job of the Electricity Board to sell electricity. And the commune settle their accounts. There are self-respecting, responsible people here, you know, Sergeant. Don't hold it against them that some of them have nowhere else to live and work. Jack Mosley doesn't."

"Yes, but good Heavens, look at this—"

Beamish was stooping to inspect the power-point.

"This is a pre-war two-pin. Obsolete: industrial archaeology. What are the chances that they'd have carried a plug to fit this?"

"They'd be sure to have had a multi-purpose adapter. They seem to have been a pretty efficient bunch."

"Or batteries, of course—power-packs. But they'd have needed a good supply to last the night."

But then his eye caught something on the floor.

"Just come and shine your torch on this, Miss Harrison."

"Deirdre—"

"Just come and shine your torch."

He picked up something, two or three small things, she could not see what. He straightened himself up, brought little plastic envelopes from an inside pocket and wrote labels for them.

"Of course, my name's only Watson," she said.

"Two broken match-sticks. One little curled fragment of stranded copper wire. Have you ever seen that done—when you have an appliance and no plug? You strip the ends of the wire and fix them into the sockets with matches or whittled bits of wood. Extremely dangerous, and I don't recommend you ever try it."

"I'd never have got that."

"And it doesn't look as if I'm going to get the names of the people you came here to check up on," he said.

She shrugged her shoulders.

"I can tell you now it wasn't them. A tape-recording of a gang-bang? Improvisations when a plug won't fit? Not their class at all. Besides, they're strictly local. This was an outside job. I'm sure of that now."

"Outsiders who must have known the potential of this place. So they must have talked to someone local."

The sense of this appealed to her.

"Why are you only a sergeant?" she asked him.

"Never mind about that. We need to know who told our chums that this was a good place to lager up."

"I'll find that out for you."

"You'll put me in a position to find out for myself."

"Oh, God! What it is not to be trusted!"

"I have to watch points," he said. "I'm answerable to superiors."

"Superiors? Jack Mosley?" She laughed. "Jack would leave it to me. Be only too glad to."

"I'll tell you what. Take me to see these friends of yours. I'll let you be present throughout."

"That," she said, "would be what is known as pissing in the milk. Two other bastards who'd never trust me again. Why don't you do what Mosley would—give me a time-limit? You can't be everywhere at once."

Every time she had mentioned Mosley's name, she had wielded it like a lethal weapon.

"What sort of a time-limit?"

"Midday tomorrow."

"Far too long."

"Eleven o'clock."

"Make it half past ten."

"Done!" she said. "Where shall I find you?"

"That's going to be your problem. And if you've got anything worth reporting, you'll find the answer."

He followed her tail-lamps out of Lower Marldale and up the lower reaches of the valley. But within ten minutes she was out of his sight.

As soon as he arrived back in the village he pulled up in the square and made for the telephone kiosk. It was the first opportunity he had had to ask Central Records if any of their clients were known to make a habit of sexual intercourse immediately after committing murder. He had some difficulty in getting through, and even more in finding his way to the sub-department most likely to have such uncommonplace information on short-notice tap. Then the line was so bad that he had to shout, and detached phrases escaped through the missing panes of the booth, much to the interest of a gang of Marldale adolescents who were gathered round their cycles a few yards away.

"Leaped into the nearest bed as soon as they'd strung somebody up—*modus operandi*—anything you've got—chap who gets an erection when he sees somebody snuffing it."

"I'll put you on to Sergeant Barker."

Sergeant Barker was a woman, which resurrected the latent puritan in Beamish, and caused him to seek a fresh phraseology.

"It seems that some people are inspired to procreation by the sight of death."

"What the hell are you talking about?"

Beamish threw all hope of euphemism to the Marldale skies.

"We've a case here of a couple who got straight on the job within a minute or two of doing a murder."

"People up your way must need education in the proper use of leisure," she said. "I'll put you through to the Inspector."

Whereupon he lost the line and had to dial afresh.

"Who are you?" the Inspector asked him.

Beamish announced his credentials.

"But we've dealt with this. An hour ago. We had an Inspector Moses on. Told him we'll come back to him in the morning."

Depressed, Beamish came out of the kiosk into the cold night air. What was Mosley playing at? It was unusual for him to do a job himself after delegating it—a rarity, in any case, for him to tackle anything at all through an established channel. Beamish became aware that there was human activity at the further side of the square. The Upper Marldale Good Companions, all eight of them, were issuing forth from the Community Centre at the end of a Bingo session. A familiar voice among the shuffling ancients caused

Beamish to cross the road. Had Mosley been filling in an idle hour succumbing to his reckless gambler's streak?

But no: it was the caretaker of the Centre that Mosley had gone in to buttonhole: a one-armed little man whose torso went through an arc of sixty degrees with every stride that his right leg took.

"Just hang on to anything that anybody brings and pass it to me when I drop in. There might be the odd letter. Everything will all be regularized in the fullness of time, and I dare say you'll get something on paper about it within a month or so. In any case, I'll see you're not the loser."

"I know you will, Mr. Mosley."

It was evident that the little cripple was one of Mosley's devotees. Beamish saw that a roughly cut oblong of cardboard had been drawing-pinned to the front door. INCIDENT ROOM. The caretaker locked up for the night.

Mosley caught sight of Beamish and sidled along to him.

"Time we knocked off for the day, I think, Sergeant."

Beamish had not made up his mind which of his two leading troubles to broach first: a politely impersonal but unequivocal complaint about the inefficiency of Mosley's duplicating the call to the CRO; or a closely argued justification of his negligence in entrusting a confidential and highly sensitive enquiry to a not very prepossessing social worker.

"What's the time, anyway?" Mosley asked and an obliging member of the gang of youths raised the frame of his cycle, pedalled furiously, and played the beam of his dynamo-driven private searchlight on to the dial of the church clock.

"Oh, my God!" Mosley said. "Oh dear, oh dear, oh dear! That's done it! That's something we could have managed very well without. I can see this bringing us no end of complications."

The clock in the tower had stopped again.

Chapter Eighteen

Detective-Superintendent Grimshaw sat at his breakfast-table with a stack of newspapers fifteen inches deep. He had an arrangement with his newsagent for the delivery of a cross-section of the nation's press whenever matters affecting his sector of law and order had achieved front-page status. If there was one thing that Grimshaw could not stand, it was to arrive in an office lined with the silent smirks of those who were ahead of him in their reading of his more spiteful critics.

There was a photograph of Mosley and Deirdre Harrison together in the Upper Marldale Square: an unfortunate juxtaposition of faces, that. CID LEANS HEAVILY ON WITCHCRAFT proclaimed one trusted organ. *Behind dour village walls*, said another, *seethes a cauldron of sex and alleged corruption*. Very careful in their use of that word *alleged*, Grimshaw always noticed, though they didn't seem to think that *sex* needed any qualifying adjective.

Some editors featured Herbert Garside's footpath. One mentioned Ned Suddaby's field. Every one made a great deal of charmed darts, expiring cabbages, frustrated hens and the stay-away instincts of the community's omniscient cats. It amused Grimshaw to reflect on what conception of everyday life in Upper Marldale might be gained by the general reader who was personally unacquainted with the Pennines.

And what the blazes was all this about?—Grimshaw had so far heard nothing of the Trixie Lowther angle:

DOORMAN'S WIDOW WAS HITLER'S FRIEND

Daughter of a once well-known brewing family, Trixie Lowther may have been injudicious in her nineteen-thirties friendships with leading Nazis. But she paid for her ill-wisdom by long wartime internment in the Reich, and even after the outbreak of peace, was for a long time held by MI5 before her final exoneration on potential charges as a renegade.

Only in her marriage to quiet, gentle-mannered Henry Cater, doorman at the British Embassy in Moscow, did she find ultimate happiness.

Long-widowed, Beatrice Cater has ended her days hanging from a beam in a picturesque tollhouse in a fell village well-known to walkers. Where will the tangled roots of Mrs. Cater's troubled past lead Detective-Inspector Mosley?

Craggy, unruffled, laconic—known locally as Crafty Jack—Inspector Mosley confidently expects to announce an arrest some time today. But the question being asked round every Marldale hearth tonight is: will Priscilla Bladon get there first?

The references, to MI5, to Cater's Christian name, to his posting in Moscow and to a nickname that no one had ever applied to Mosley before, were all editorial embellishments aimed thoughtfully at the contentment of the readership. Grimshaw also felt that there were other features in this narrative which might be straining truth. But this was surely all to the good. He thought he deserved to congratulate himself on the wisdom (by this time he believed that it was his) that had left Mosley in sole charge up in the hills. Mosley was certainly digging things up. And attention was certainly being well and truly diverted from Councillor Harry Whitcombe.

Only one newspaper—the *Morning Herald*—had been put to bed so late that its observant reporter had been able to report that the Upper Marldale church clock had stopped again.

HERALD CHALLENGES COVEN ran the headline.

Can the coven start the clock again? The *Morning Herald* issues this challenge to the Marldale witches. Can they,

under stringently refereed conditions, start the Marldale
clock without approaching within a fifty yards' radius of the
church tower? Should they succeed, we propose to buy and
donate to them a field which has for a long time been a
bone of contention in the parish, together with a pavil-
ion, goal-posts, a gang-mower and basic recreation-ground
equipment.

All to the good, Grimshaw told himself. Any red her-
ring across the misty flanks of Marldale was welcome, giving
both time and privacy to the priority business of mixing a
bottle for Councillor Whitcombe.

There was one brief message from Mosley on the Detective-Superintendent's desk. *Incident Room in Marldale
Community Centre.* Mosley really did seem to be using his
loaf at last.

Grimshaw gave the Assistant Chief Constable's secretary time to get her coat off, and spoke to her one minute
after nine. By ten-thirty he was in the ACC's room.

"Good press, I'd say, on the whole, wouldn't you?" the
ACC said.

"A lively one, certainly."

"I must say there do seem to be unexpected complexi-
ties. Thank God Mosley has a clear mind."

"So has Beamish. Between them, I believed they are
going to keep people occupied."

"And I take it that you haven't been wasting your time,
either, Tom?"

"No, sir—"

Grimshaw produced papers—which the ACC did not
want to see—and briefly outlined the three cases which he
believed worth following up: the hypermarket, the sports
centre, and the Evenlode home. The ACC looked extremely grave.

"But these aren't the three cases the CEO referred to
the DPP, Tom. I deliberately didn't tell you what they
were, because I felt it would absolutely clinch matters if
you were to put your finger on them yourself."

"These others give us additional ammunition, surely."

"That's as may be. The question is, do we want additional ammunition? Oh, I know every little helps. But we don't want to complicate matters, do we? Simplify, Tom—wherever possible, simplify."

"Simplicity hasn't seemed to me to be the hallmark of anything concerned with this case so far," Grimshaw said, but the ACC did not appear to have heard this. It was as if an additional problem was more than he could sustain. He tapped on his desk four times with his finger-nails, a sure sign that he was distraught, and continued to wear the most extreme face of gravity of which he was capable.

"I think we'd better take this to the Chief," he said at last.

The Chief made them very welcome, creating the feeling that he had been pining all morning for the company of colleagues.

"Old Mosley certainly seems to be jollying things along in Marldale," he said.

"Oh, yes. I don't think we can complain of lack of incident."

"One thing has worried me about what I've been reading in this morning's papers."

Only one thing—?

"Perhaps you can tell me, Grimshaw: is any detail of what has been published true in any respect, or is it all a figment of Mosley's imagination?"

"There are cross-currents," Grimshaw said on the spur of the moment, and realized that he had hit upon a phrase that would stand him in good stead in many a future contingency.

"And what's the problem?"

"Detective-Superintendent Grimshaw has unearthed cases additional to those referred by the Chief Executive Officer," the ACC said.

"Oh, dear."

He looked solemnly at Grimshaw.

"We have to be careful, you know, Grimshaw, very careful indeed. We have to distinguish between investigation and muck-raking. We have to dredge the bottom of the pond, as it were, without making it look as if we're stirring things up."

He held out his hand for the papers he could see Grimshaw was holding, and, unlike his Assistant, he did read them. He read them from beginning to end, once or twice looking back to check cross-references.

"I think you'd better leave these with me."

Grimshaw went back downstairs, feeling as if his day had suddenly been emptied. But there was by now a sufficiency of routine aggro on his desk and he soon found himself in the familiar role of improvising ways in which distant colleagues might escape from temporary impasses. It was not until half past three in the afternoon that the Chief's secretary rang him. The Chief thought that it might serve a useful purpose, might clear the air, as it were, if he went and had a little chat with the Chief Executive Officer.

The CEO saw him at once, though "Tod" Hunter's was by common agreement the busiest desk in County Hall. Everything about him spoke of the family man. Photographs of his wife and children stood in frames within his constant line of vision. He wore what was obviously a hand-knitted cardigan, and although he gave his staff considerable latitude in the matter of casual dress, was always himself in a suit: he was of stock size, and generally wore off-the-peg clothes. Hunter was a solicitor, held a diploma in public administration, was an Associate of the Society of Secretaries. His speech still retained a noticeable touch of the locality—an expert could have identified his home-corner. Grimshaw had met him often enough—in the staff canteen and at obligatory functions—but this was the first time they had worked closely together on anything. The two men took to each other.

Hunter listened, nodding with quiet, unspectacular agreement, while Grimshaw recited his three cases.

"Yes. I knew about these of course, and I'd wondered. The pattern is the same. The Council sells land—and the buyer does substantially better out of the deal than the Council does. But you see there are dozens of other cases, also put through during Councillor Whitcombe's chairmanship, that are transparently above reproach. There are times when land has to be sold. There are other times, much less frequent nowadays, when land has to be bought. In either case, both buyer and seller hope to profit. Sometimes one of them doesn't—and sometimes the one that doesn't is the Council. In your instances the Council didn't—but the only common feature in them is Councillor Whitcombe's committee. It's the same with the cases that I brought forward. Let me tell you what they were."

There was a hill-top sold off dirt-cheap to a syndicate that wanted it for a country club. Only after the deeds had changed hands did the Ministry of Defence suddenly want it for the masts and radar dishes of its early-warning system.

High towering masts featured on another patch, too. Again, it was regarded as little more than waste land. It was looked on as the folly of an earlier Council ever to have tied up capital in it in the first place. They were lucky to sell it—for a song: except that within two years the Post Office saw its potential for a relay station in their internal communications system.

And finally there was an area of edge-of-town land that in more prosperous years had been ear-marked for overspill and industrial estate—developments that had become a fantasy in the paralysis of recession. It was disposed of as "investment"—amid the angry voices of some who wanted to know why their own Council could not have sat tight on a long-term gamble too. They might not have had to wait too long, because the site was now a privately owned heli-port, with expanding air-taxi services to Manchester, the West Riding, the East Midlands, Birmingham and Tyneside. Already there were tenders in for a hotel and shopping-mall.

"It looks as if history's forever repeating itself," Hunter said. "But is it? And if it is—prove it. The beneficiary was not the same in any two deals we've mentioned."

"The only common ground is Harry Whitcombe?"

"Who as chairman has the best entitlement in the world to be in on everything. Whenever I speak of Councillor Whitcombe, by the way, I mean Councillor Whitcombe plus associates. But don't ask me who they are. He doesn't meet them in pubs across the road from County Hall after committee meetings. It's on a vastly bigger scale than that—it has to be. More likely Marbella or the Bahamas."

"Tell me who the beneficiaries were."

Hunter did. Four of them were companies, but neither these nor the individuals concerned meant anything to Grimshaw.

"You've run your eye down the directors' lists?"

"I've done everything that's obvious—and a good deal that's devious and remote. No joy."

Hunter pushed his chair back from the desk and looked at Grimshaw with a tired smile.

"Joy, did I say? Do you think I'm getting joy out of this? The intoxication of the chase? You don't look to me as if you suffer from a surfeit of that, either, Grimshaw. I sometimes think this job's simply making me bloody-minded. Maybe I saw too many films about the Mounties when I was a boy. Hunter gets his man. I feel bad about this, Grimshaw, that's the dried-out truth of it."

He opened a drawer, offered Grimshaw a cigarette from a wood-carved box. Neither man smoked.

"I'm a well-salaried man, Grimshaw, because I've always worked hard. I'm the best-paid man in this block of offices. And where does it go? I still have to do sums at the end of every month. I run an Escort—I used to cycle in to work until I was in my thirties. I didn't have colour television till two years ago. I have four children. We always said we'd have four children. They go to state schools, because every penny I can save is for their future. Because when it comes to seeing them through university, I shall be trapped in an income bracket that will have me soaked for every shekel. In my early sixties I shall cash in on a couple of endowment policies—if I haven't yet had my coronary. And I look round and see these buggers heading for Bermuda in their yachts—safari parks in Kenya—Sri Lanka—"

He subsided.

"I'm not jealous, Grimshaw. I have a thing about visible justice, that's all. I like to see a fair relationship between effort put in and plums pulled out. When a man gets his halo from the hold he has over the electorate, I don't like to see the electorate taken to the cleaners. That's why I want to nail this villain. And it's over to you, now, so thank God I can get on with something else. Of course, if there's any mortal thing you need in the way of help from this office—"

"I would like to see your full file on the transactions we've been talking about."

"You shall. In fact I anticipated and sent down to Registry for them as soon as your Chief had spoken to me this morning. So they should be ready waiting for you."

He picked up his phone and spoke to the woman in his outer office. Then frowned.

"I'm sorry. I'll get them to you as fast as I can. There seems to have been some hitch."

Chapter Nineteen

It meant an early start for Beamish, because for one thing, as he had expected, Mosley had nobbled him to do his chauffeuring, which added three quarters of an hour to the first leg of his journey. And for another, Mosley had insisted that they must be on Herbert Garside's land by seven.

So they were pulling out of Bradburn while Grimshaw still had an hour of restless and unfortifying sleep in front of him, and they were climbing into droplet mists while sheep were still under the illusion that no motorist was likely to be on the road.

Marldale Nab Farm was a mile out of Upper Marldale, on a prominence that overlooked the first dip of the dale itself. It was true that there was a right of way through Herbert Garside's fields, but as a link it was vital neither to society nor commerce, since it went nowhere that could not be more conveniently reached. Once a year the Footpaths Association sent a member to walk along its length, thereby establishing its continued usage, but no one in Upper Marldale would have dreamed of treading it. It was only when Bert Garside appeared to be denying it them that they held a public meeting and brought out cogent reasons why they could not live without it.

Beamish and Mosley trod it. They had not taken many paces before Beamish saw the wisdom of Mosley's insistence that they bring their gumboots. One length of the path was a minor watercourse, inches deep at certain seasons of the year—and this was one of those seasons. Beamish made a detour and found, in different places, three lengths of old guttering that at first sight looked as if they had been casually discarded. But when he examined them in context,

114

he saw that they had been skilfully placed so as to direct a further two-pennyworth to the downward flow.

Mosley seemed unsurprised, in fact uninterested.

"Shouldn't bother my head too much over that, lad. We know he's doing it. We've been told so, haven't we?"

As if the word of any Marldale informant was a sacred revelation.

They found a tree, a scarred and arthritic hawthorn, freshly broken from a jagged stump and lying across the path at one of its narrowest stretches between walls. The marks of the axe were clearly visible.

"Not done by squirrels," Mosley said.

They found a stile that had been stopped up, the new coping secured by recent mortar.

"He doesn't seem to be making much effort to conceal what he's up to," Beamish said.

"Why should he? He wants everybody to know that this is an awkward way to come—and everybody does."

Beamish stopped for breath and looked around all the compass points. A boundary across a dew-pond was declared by the head and foot of an old brass bed-stead. There was a mess of soggy wool and bones that had been a still-born lamb. There was a short length of electrified fencing that was connected to nothing at either end.

"How does a man make a living out of this?" Beamish asked.

"Ask Herbert Garside's accountant. In fact, HM Inspector of Taxes would give his ears to know the half of what Herbert Garside's accountant knows. He's a good farmer, is Herbert, has a good eye for an animal."

"But he has to take the rough with the smooth. And it seems to me there's a hell of a lot of rough about here."

"Herbert holidays in Gran Canaria. He's been to the Costa Brava and Sorrento, but he prefers the Canaries. Even in years when the Inland Revenue have had to bring forward his last year's losses."

They were close to the farmhouse now and arrived at the stretch that Upper Marldale had the most to complain about: thirty yards between a field-gate and the milking-parlour which he was accused of swilling down before the passage of his herd. It was the sort of morass that sucked a man's wellingtons off, and it was in prime condition at the moment because the herd was actually passing. Mosley waited for the last slow, slobbering beast to go through into the yard. A fifty-year-old man in a leather jerkin was standing arms akimbo, waiting to close the gate.

"Morning, Jack."

"Morning, Bert."

"To what do I owe this pleasure?"

"The pleasure's one-sided," Mosley said, indicating the slough.

"I don't know what's got into folk. They ought to know farms are mucky places."

"And should they expect stiles to be stopped and mortared?"

"Folk can still climb them, if they want to cross badly enough."

"Yes, well, some of us do. We want to know what's going on."

Mosley had Beamish precede him into the yard. Garside closed the gate.

"If this were on the telly, I'd ask to see your warrant."

"Well, it isn't. And we haven't got one. And we're here."

Garside looked into the milking-parlour. Each cow had gone in leisurely fashion into her accustomed stall.

"You'd better make it smartish then. I've this lot to milk."

By way of answer, Mosley turned his back on him and stumped stiff-legged in his gumboots down to a gated track that led round to the front of the house. At the back the farm had the neglected appearance of an old Norse longhouse. On the other side some early-nineteenth-century yeoman had pushed out a mock-Palladian double front so that his wife could have her drawing-room and dining-room. The lawn, which was going to have to be laid afresh, was piled with builder's materials: a good deal of brise, lengths of piping and stacks of glazed slabs.

"So what are you building here, Bert? Tractor-shed or swimming-pool?"

"Both," Garside said.

Beamish noticed that he had made no effort to dissimulate to Mosley.

"What the hell do you want with a swimming-pool on Marldale Nab, Bert? Your knackers will shrivel up."

"They bloody won't. Because I shan't be putting as much as a bloody toe-nail in it. Anyway, it's going to be heated. The youngsters want it—for when we have the Young Farmers here. And it'll add to the value of the property if ever I have to sell up."

"You'll want a boiler-house, a filter unit. You'll need planning permission."

"You don't for a tractor-shed."

"So you're hoping that one will mask the other? You're making trouble for yourself, Bert. It will go on for years."

"By which time I shall have my pool."

"Why don't you keep ducks in it? Then you can say it's purely for agricultural purposes. Honestly, Bert, you'll save yourself years of argy-bargy, by going through the channels."

"That's what it's all about, Jack. I can't afford to go through the bloody channels. I can't raise the premium."

"Why don't you ask for a swimming-pool on your Supplementary Benefits, Bert? Of course you can afford it. The fee's only nominal."

"That shows how little you know. Do you know how many palms I'd have to cross to get this through in less than bloody years? How many times would the plans be chucked back at me, by committee after committee, because they don't like this tile or that keyhole? It starts at the bloody bottom, Jack. It starts with the clerks. It starts when you hand your papers in, if you don't want them stuck for ever at the bottom of the pile."

"Which clerks?"

"Nay, Jack. You're not going to ham-string me with that one. I only know what's happened to other people."

"Which other people?"

"You're not going to catch me that way, either."

"Why don't you behave like a model citizen, Bert—put in a complaint, if you think you've got one."

"Because I want a swimming-pool. Within the next two years. As simple as that. The Old Chap up There helps those who help themselves, I've always been given to understand."

Mosley turned to Beamish.

"Treasure this moment, Sergeant. You've just had a front-row seat at an exhibition piece of Marldale thinking. Well, thank you, Bert. I've been. I've seen. I know."

They started off back down the obstacle course, were in sight of the blocked stile when they saw an unathletic female figure rolling over the top of the wall. She picked herself up out of the wet grass and commented on the situation in terms which made Mosley pretend to cover his face—and Beamish stare away at an angle. She had discarded yesterday's bib-and-brace and was wearing a long, loose, orange-turtlenecked sweater that deprived her of what shape she had.

"Morning, Deirdre. This your daily Keep Fit course?"

She repeated the tenor of her previous comments, though in a bowdlerized, less vitriolic spirit.

"It's gone like wild fire round Marldale that you've come up here, so I've come after you. Because this is important."

"Good," Mosley said.

"Sergeant Beamish asked me last night to find something out for him. I've found it out."

"Let's go down to the bottom of this field, get that corner of wall between us and the draught."

"I was hoping to keep personalities out of this," she said, when they had found stones to sit on. "But I know now that that's impossible. I'm not daft. This is too big. Merle Cox and Kevin Kenyon. But I'd ask you to do what you can to keep their names out of printer's ink. The Coxes and the Kenyons are the Montagues and Capulets of Little Hawdale."

"I know them," Mosley said. "Their parents and grandparents, anyway. I couldn't put names and faces to all the kids."

"Well, you'll know then we don't want more ructions than happen in Hawdale in any normal week. And Merle and Kevin aren't kids any more. He's nineteen, she's seventeen. They've been going steady for eighteen months, and when their glandular secretions get out of hand, they tend to home in on the Old Glasshouse. That's all right," she said, catching the look on Beamish's face. "She's on the pill. I've seen to that. And don't look so shocked, Sergeant. While they're stuck on each other, he isn't catching a dose in Bradburn, Saturday nights, and she isn't hawking her greens in Little Hawdale churchyard."

"You mean they're the couple that spent the night in that disgusting little cubicle?"

"No, no. No, no. Not them. But they know who did. At least, I'm pretty sure that three people they met are the ones. And they gave me an interesting description."

"Where and when did they come across this bunch?"

"Smoky Joe's, the night before they booked in at the Glasshouse."

Smoky Joe's was a cafe on the Marldale-Pringle road —or, at least, on a forgotten loop of it that had been superseded by a stretch of dual carriageway. Having lost its heavy-goods clientele, the place now catered frankly for the amateur Hell's Angels of the district, for whom it provided Coke, hamburgers, chips, tomato sauce ad lib and the comfort of a juke-box.

"You don't see many strangers in Smoky's, and these three were asking Joe if he had accommodation, which shows how green they were."

She looked as if she thought that the squalor of Joe's was beyond the experience of Beamish and Mosley.

"It frightens me sometimes," she said, "what these kids know. No one would put Merle Cox up as the Brain of Pringle, even after three years in the Remedial stream. When she left school she could only write one English word: *to*. And she spelled that *ot*. But she remembers things she's heard people like her grandmother say. "You know," she said. "If you want to know how old a woman is, it isn't her fizzog you look at. It's her hands. Look at the veins at the bottom of her fingers, the cracks and wrinkles between them. This woman was old: thirty if she was a day.""

"And Kevin Kenyon had his eyes peeled, too. 'There was one of them,' he said, 'I didn't know at first whether it was a feller or a tart, they all had that much eye-shadow on. But then when he uncrossed his legs, you could see the shape of his tool under his jeans. Like a bloody great banana, it was. And he had these dimpled scars under the corner of his jaw.' That ought to be something for you people to go on. I know what these scars were. There was a girl in college who had them: surgery for TB glands, when she was a kid."

"It's more than we've had to go on up to now," Beamish said. "But it's still far from proof that they went anywhere near the Tollhouse."

"They asked Merle and Kevin where there was to doss round here. So they recommended the Glasshouse, and told them to tell Joe Murray they had sent them."

"That only gets them as far as the cubicle."

"And there's one more thing. When they got up to leave Smoky Joe's, these three picked something up from beside one of their chairs—a radio cassette-recorder-player, wrapped up in dirty newspaper and tied round with grotty string. But Kevin reckons to know a bit about that sort of thing, largely through looking at them in shop-windows. He said that this was a special job: stereo, four speakers, must have cost a small fortune. The girl was nursing a black poodle, too."

"Useful pointer," Beamish said, "but it doesn't put anyone in the dock yet."

Deirdre was impatient with his professional caution.

"It points the right bloody way, I would have thought. I mean, it makes sense to me. Any stranger hanging about for a day and night in Marldale at this time of year would stand out like a two-shilling piece up a chimney-sweep's bum. The only way not to be noticed would be to go rock-bottom and stick around with the rock-bottom set. I think that was clever."

"But not clever enough," Mosley said. "Thank you, Deirdre. I think you may have put us on to something."

When they got back to Upper Marldale, they saw from the top of the High Street that someone was hammering bad-temperedly at the door of the Community Centre. Beamish was for hurrying, but Mosley held him by the shoulder.

"Don't let him get us excited."

It was Major Hindle. They knew at once he was uncomfortable about whatever he had come for, because he started making heavy jokes from the outset.

"You call this an Incident Room? There's nobody here."

"There's a caretaker. He'll take any messages."

"Old Hardcastle? He's as deaf as a post."

"You'll be complaining next about the lack of incidents," Mosley said.

He tapped gently with his knuckles and Hardcastle pulled the door open at once, the upper part of his body at its midway point between nearly upright and almost parallel with the ground.

"There's no need to break the panels in."

The grey wooden floor was embellished with loops and overlapping circles where Hardcastle's last token wielding of his mop had been allowed to dry out. One of the heavy plum-coloured curtains on the diminutive platform was hanging from only three of its dozen brass rings, and the main furnishing was a dozen or so baize-coloured cardtables. There was a chill in the room, as if its four walls somehow managed to perpetuate the lowest mean minimum temperature of the region.

"Do you think we might have some light?" Mosley asked.

"I'll see what I can do."

They went and sat down at one of the card-tables. Hindle looked as if he had been losing sleep. He was as small a man as Mosley, not an inch taller than him—but Mosley was at least fleshed out. And he was wearing a thirty-year-old greatcoat of heavy herringbone pattern into which he seemed to be visibly shrinking as he sat.

"Inspector—there are one or two things I feel I ought to clear up."

He looked desperately unhappy. His was the surrender of a man who had come to lay his whole persona, such as it was, on the line.

"Inspector, I'd far rather, far rather, if there's anything else that you feel you have to talk to me about, that you don't come to the cottage to do so. I mean, don't think for a moment I'm trying to dictate your approach to your work, but try not to, if you can possibly avoid it, if you see what I mean, there's a good fellow."

Beamish and Mosley were both sufficiently steeped in the manners of men to remain frozen, waiting for what might come next.

"I mean, I'm not saying that I have anything particularly to be proud of, but by the same token, I don't regard myself as a moral reprobate. Life might perhaps have been easier if certain things hadn't happened, but they have happened and one has to take what comes in train. But they have a saying in these parts, 'What the eye don't see, the heart don't grieve,' and I've always said to myself, that's not a bad motto for a man. What I am getting at is this: I'm not making moral excuses but the only thing, to my mind, that makes an offence inexcusable is if a third party gets hurt in the process. Now the little woman, you see, can't be hurt by what she doesn't know—and I wouldn't have her hurt at any price. We are in the twilight of our days, Inspector, shadows lengthening and that sort of thing. I do not want us to spend our last years in misery and recrimination."

It was possible to look at him and picture the hours and days of guilt and unforgiveness in their cottage on the hill: Mrs. Hindle asking herself where she had gone wrong, the Major's psyche sapped even of the creative urge to make a walking-stick.

"It all started, you see, the year the war ended. I was the Commandant, as you know, of a transit camp for politically sensitive internees, among them Miss Lowther, as she then was. I didn't know any detail, of course, but there was obviously a lot of string-pulling and attempted string-pulling going on behind the scenes, the Lowthers not wanting the family named dragged through any more mud than it was caked in already. My confidential instructions were to make sure that she did not escape and, that apart, to make her as comfortable as circumstances permitted. Well, you can see how things happened. I was still a youngish man, not past my physical prime, she was not unattractive and hadn't had the society of a cultivated Englishman for years."

No comment.

"I know it was unpardonable, but if I hadn't slept with her, I dare say my Company Sergeant Major would have.

I'm telling you all this, Inspector, making a clean breast of it all, so that you'll see when I come to the end of this sorry story that I have missed nothing out."

At that moment something odd seemed to happen to the Community Centre. It became illuminated by a single forty-watt bulb hanging somewhere among the roof-girders. Hardcastle had remembered to switch it on—or had succeeded after experiments in doing so.

"Of course, if it had ever come to light, the repercussions would have rattled from Aldershot to Chelsea. Even now—"

"I wouldn't worry too much about that," Mosley said, taking pity on him at last. "I can't tell you without the book how it goes, but there must be a Statute of Limitations, even on courts martial. This was only just short of half a century ago—"

"It isn't that, old chap. It would mean the loss of everything I've ever worked and stood for. They still remember now and then to invite me to a Mess Night at the Depot. I have more than once been honoured with a place on the podium at a ceremonial march past. Then there's the Royal British Legion. I've been working for years to get a branch going in Marldale."

"Yes, well, I see your point of view," Mosley said. "And I see nothing up to now that should isolate you under the arc-lights. Always provided, of course, that we don't have to keep coming back to you every day for further information."

"But that's the whole point, Inspector Mosley. I am here to see your sergeant write down in his notebook every damned thing that I know, every detail I can remember. You see, five years ago, I happened to come across Mrs. Cater in Bradcaster. She was up in the district house-hunting. It stands to sense I was interested to see her—old times, damned good laugh, took her into the Feathers for a gin. And you know how your tongue sometimes carries you away, you don't think of consequences. I happened to tell her the Old Tollhouse was on the market, just the place, I told her, for a sculptress, which was what she said she was nowadays. Didn't think another damned thing about it—till she bloody well turned up here. And then—"

And then she had blackmailed him into sleeping with her. It was not necessary for either side to crystallize it out in unpalatable words. Beamish looked at the Major without blinking; in this case he was becoming accustomed to the images of grotesque physical relationships.

"If it hadn't been me, it would have been the milkman or the window-cleaner," Hindle said.

"I'm more interested in the times you took her to Bradburn in your car," Mosley interrupted.

"I'm coming to that."

"How many trips did you make?"

"Three in all."

"And the dates?"

"Couldn't be sure at this range, old man. First was a month ago, then another a week later to the day. Then a third about ten days after that. I'm surprised my little woman didn't start getting suspicious."

"And each time, Mrs. Cater went to the County Offices?"

"Only on the first two occasions. Perhaps if I were to tell the story chronologically—?"

"Not a bad idea sometimes, Major. Did she give you any idea what she was going to County Hall for?"

"Oh, yes—she prattled away like a burst pipe. Always did. One got into the way of not listening. It goes without saying that she tried to involve me. It was all about this field, and this footpath, and bribery and corruption that she reckoned was going on in high quarters. As if I'd want to get my fingers burned by dabbling in things like that!"

"But she felt she was definitely on to something?"

"She *always* felt she was on to something. Whatever else you can say about Bea Cater, she never lacked confidence. Even in her most crack-brained schemes she was confident from the word go. I've even known her to change her mind in mid-stream and be equally confident against what she had been saying two minutes previously. A funny woman, Inspector. Not unintelligent—but hare-brained."

"Bribery and corruption?"

"She'd somehow got the idea into her head that you had to pay through the nose, all along the line, if you wanted planning permission for anything from a dog kennel to your own multi-storey car park. Otherwise you were subject to months of delay at every stage. She did tell me how many tens of thousands of applications they have outstanding. But ten quid here, twenty there, fifty there, and you'd got the builders in tomorrow week. What's more, she seemed to think that Harry Whitcombe was in this up to the elbows. Harry Whitcombe! As transparently sincere a councillor as ever sat in Bradburn or Pringle. Damn it—the man has the Territorial Decoration."

"So at what level did she propose to enter the fray?"

"She had that all worked out. Senior clerical, in the first instance. Poor devil—young fellow who runs the outer office of the Planning Department. She said she wasn't going to waste time on counter-clerks—and she wasn't going to wait all day for this young fiddler to declare himself, either. What was his name? Roger Something-or-other— Roger Smallwood, Norton, Carruthers—something like that. She had a great-nephew serving his time in some drawing-office and she'd got him to sketch out plans for an extension to her studio. She took these in, handed them over, insisted on seeing somebody senior to the first two minions who appeared, told Roger What's-his-name that if any sweeteners were needed anywhere up the ladder, money was no object as far as she was concerned. Naturally, he wasn't going to touch it with a boat-hook. Told her this was a public department, every file and every stage open to democratic scrutiny, and her plans would go forward through the machine without let and without favour. I had it in the car all the way back to Marldale. My ears were ringing with it. She seemed to think that the most vicious thing about young Roger was his refusal to play ball."

At this juncture old Hardcastle came shuffling and oscillating into the room with a tray bearing the largest and most battered-looking metal teapot that Beamish had ever seen: it must have held a gallon.

"I thought perhaps you gentlemen—"

The tea was thickly orange in colour and bitter from the years of deposits in the pot.

"Well, a week later, Bea Cater nabbed me again and wanted another trip to Bradburn. She hinted darkly that from some source or other she had got on to something else

to young Roger's disadvantage, and this time she really was
going to nail him. Now I'd seen enough of Bea Cater in my
time to know that when she was reduced to dropping dark
hints, it meant either that she had no information at all—
or that she was merely trying to be intriguing, and the next
thing one knew one was up to the ears in something or
other. It paid not even to ask questions—and I didn't. But
when she came out of the Offices, she was beaming like a
summer's day. I thought perhaps that she'd tripped Roger
up at last—but he'd given her something. I can only suppose that she'd worn him out under weight and spate of
words, and that he'd dug something complex and innocuous
out just to get rid of her. It was in one of those large buff
envelopes that they use for shunting files about in—a brand-
new one, and I remember saying to myself, there's no wonder the rates are what they are.

" 'I've got something here,' she said, 'that's going to
set Bradburn and Marldale on fire.'

"But I staunchly refused to ask her what it was, and
although that wouldn't in the normal run of things have
stopped her from telling me, she got annoyed with me,
because she said I was anti-social. We parted in a definite
atmosphere. Then ten days later she begged to be taken to
Bradburn again. I asked her when her own car was going
to be back on the road, and it seemed that she had become
so peeved with the people who were supposed to be getting
it up to MoT scratch for her that she had had it towed to
a different garage and had started the whole process again
from square one."

And this time, Mrs. Cater had not been able to resist
telling the Major what was in her buff envelope, although
he repeated emphatically that he did not want to know. It
was a desk diary, she said, not a principal's, but a secretary's
desk diary—a top secretary's desk diary—the sort of diary
in which she had made, for her own guidance, notes of the
kind that her boss would have been cautious about committing to paper: like certain trips he had made, appointments to meet certain people—things that he might not
have cared to broadcast among some of the watch-dogs on
his committees. It was, in fact, Councillor Harry Whitcombe's personal assistant's desk diary of some years ago,

in which she had scribbled odd reminders to herself about where Whitcombe was likely to be on given days.

"I know three women in Upper Marldale," Mrs. Cater had said, "who would sing incantations round a mess of pottage to get their hands on this diary."

But it was not to County Hall that she had Hindle drive her on her third visit. It was to a house on the Dales Estate, Bradburn's most patrician residential area. And she did not even allow him to know, within fifty yards in any direction, which one she was calling at. She had him put her down and wait for her at the corner of Wharfedale Avenue and Wensleydale Close. She kept him there for three quarters of an hour, and when she returned she was quite silent about where she had been and what had taken place there. In fact she was altogether subdued, which made Hindle think that something had happened to cast her down.

"In fact I came to the very satisfying conclusion," Hindle said, "that just for once, dear Beatrice had met her match."

"She met her match right enough. She met it with a rope round her neck, standing on a table that had been dragged in from her studio."

"You really think there's a connection, Inspector?"

Mosley examined the back of his right hand with such intensity that it looked as if he had never seen it before.

"Let's say we have to bear the possibility in mind. Sooner or later something is going to connect with something else. I hope. Well, now, Major Hindle—is there anything else that you feel we ought to know?"

"I think that's about it, Inspector. If there's anything that you think needs clarification—"

"We'll be in touch."

"Discreetly, I implore you."

"Discreet enough to ask for discretion in return, Major. I would greatly prefer you not to discuss with anyone else the things we have talked about this morning—"

"There is really no need for you to remind me of that, Inspector."

"Otherwise somebody else in Marldale might be getting a nocturnal visit in the near future," Mosley said.

Chapter Twenty

As soon as Hindle had left them, Mosley went for a short walk round the interior of the Community Centre, looking at its few exhibits as if they held some deep-seated interest for him: an engraving of *Napoleon on the Beller-ophon*, foxed and askew; the tea-making roster of the ladies of the Dorcas Club. It was the first time that Beamish had ever seen him immersed in a thought process that did not seem to be leading to any immediate conclusion. Beamish remained respectfully silent and seated, waiting for something to be evolved. Mosley remained standing for a long time under the portrait of a Chairman of the Parish Council who had died in 1923. Then he came back, seated himself opposite Beamish at the baize-topped card-table—and stood up again to get pipe and tobacco out of his over-stuffed pockets.

"You know, Sergeant Beamish, I keep coming back in my mind to something that Priscilla Bladon said on her own premises last night. 'That lightning won't strike here again.' Always a dangerous sentiment, though in private, in this case, until now, I've been inclined to agree with her. The people who killed Beatrice Cater are professional, efficient, sophisticated killers. Carnal-minded, too, I grant you, but that goes hand in hand. To come back here and do another killing would be taking a risk at which I'd have thought they'd have jibbed. But if Harry Whitcombe's secretary's desk diary was worth killing for once, it might be vital to kill for it again."

"But who knows about the diary? Major Hindle does not know what was in it. He does not even know which house on the Dales Estate Mrs. Cater went to."

"True. But are the killers aware of that?"

"If they were in any doubt, they would surely have got rid of Hindle while they were up here liquidating Mrs. Cater."

"It was not Major Hindle I was thinking of. I was thinking of the three ladies, who were drinking Mrs. Cater's chartreuse only an hour or so before Mrs. Cater died. Mrs. Cater apparently ended up by telling them nothing. Because they could not agree on terms: that was the phrase that Miss Bladon used. But the killer—the man who commissioned the killings—cannot know that. He is bound to assume the contrary."

"So you think that our friends from the NCOs' annexe at the Glasshouse will be back?"

"I doubt it. I think they would set their price too high for a second visit. But they are not the only contract killers on the books of whichever Job Centre these people use."

But now Beamish, who was sitting with his back to the main entrance, was aware that someone else had come in. Mosley rose politely and Beamish followed example, turning to see Priscilla Bladon bearing down on them with the skirts of her outdoor coat billowing majestically. She came and sat down at their table, lifting the lid of the teapot in casual inspection.

"God! Who made that?"

"Dick Hardcastle."

"So we have competition? I've always said that man was a warlock. Jack Mosley, we're in difficulty. Now is the time for all good men and true—or, rather, for both good men and true, since there are only two of you—to come to the aid of the party."

"What's the trouble, Miss Bladon?"

"The challenge from the *Morning Herald*. Their reporter's just been round to see me, given me a memorandum of the conditions. Want to see it?"

"Not particularly. Give us a rough idea."

"The Editor of the *Herald*, a retired Commissioner of Metropolitan Police and a Senior Lecturer in Parapsychology at Brunel University are to act as adjudicators and their judgement will be final. A national security organization has guaranteed to prevent access to the church. The clock tower will be guarded inside and out by dogs."

"So starting the clock's going to be quite an achievement."

"We must get it started, Jack—on two counts we must. We can't afford to lose face. And we've got to win Ned Suddaby's field from the *Herald*, together with all the equipment they're throwing in with it."

"Shouldn't be too difficult. My guess is there's nothing much wrong with the clock. It only wants winding."

"I dare say. But who's going to get through a battalion of security men and several nests of hungry Alsatians to wind it?"

"Makes me wish I was a younger man," Mosley said.

"Do be serious, Jack. I am. Deadly serious."

"But it does need a younger man."

"A young man with more ideas than I've got at the moment."

"We're getting youngsters with all sorts of technical knowledge in the force these days," Mosley said.

Then he turned to Beamish, with the most genial and idiotic smile on his face that Beamish had seen there to date.

"Sergeant Beamish, I'm putting you in charge of getting the Upper Marldale church clock going again under the conditions prescribed by the *Morning Herald*."

Beamish opened his mouth, then decided against saying anything. He would deal with Mosley when Miss Bladon had gone.

"As soon as we leave here, Sergeant Beamish, I want you to go down to the hospital at Pringle. Mention my name in the Matron's office, and ask if you can have a sympathetic word with Peter Muller."

"Who's Peter Muller?"

"The regular Marldale clock-winder. Bear in mind that he is a very sick man, and that the Marldale clock is very dear to his heart. Do not under any circumstances allow him to think that you are usurping his seigneurial rights over the clock tower—but find out from him how to wind the clock. And give your mind to any other attendant difficulties that might occur to you. We will have another little talk about this later."

"We will indeed," Beamish said, trying not to clench his teeth.

Sometimes in the evening, the citizens of Bradburn looked up at the tower block of their controversial new County Offices and saw lights blazing from every window on the many floors. The more naive may possibly have thought that this denoted overtime devotion by faithful local-government servants. Others realized that it merely meant that the vast acreage of car park had cleared and that the cleaners had moved in, switching on everything in sight and leaving the ratepayers to face the quarterly electricity bill.

Police headquarters were not in County Hall itself but in a cold, echoing, stone-floored building that had been the pride of Bradburn when a Royal Duke had declared it open in the 1880s. From his desk, looking obliquely backwards over his left shoulder, Detective-Superintendent Grimshaw could just see a narrow triangle of the upper tier of County Hall, framed by the back of Woolworth's, the rear of the Odeon Cinema and the mock battlements and turrets of a nineteenth-century mill. He saw the cleaners' lights go on and knew that another day had passed. And what had he to show for it? Since this morning early he had been showered with the problems that his underlings in the divisions were finding insuperable. And in every case his solution had been a holding operation, an avoidance of risk, a maintaining of the comfortably familiar, a counselling to eternal patience, so that tomorrow men could hang up their outdoor clothes on their office hatstands, pick up the phones from their desks and set the whole process in motion again.

For the last twenty minutes Grimshaw had been endeavouring to comfort the Chief Inspector, Q Division, about his chronic shortage of experienced sergeants. There was nothing that Grimshaw could do about it—except wait for sergeants to gain experience. He had found at least two dozen ways of saying this—and all the while he was talking, he saw the chances diminishing of his consulting the Chief

Executive Officer before the cleaners had mopped up every other island of resistance and dislodged even the top man.

"Tod" Hunter had promised faithfully that he would contact Grimshaw before the end of the working day about the file that he had wanted him to see, and that his Registry had apparently mislaid. And the CEO had not kept his promise. So should Grimshaw take the initiative and ring the CEO? Why was it that the higher one reached in one's lifelong pursuit of promotion, the more terrifying the pettiest of decisions became? As a young and ambitious officer, Grimshaw had often wondered why all his seniors were perpetually worried men. He did not know the answer yet—but he knew that he was in danger of becoming a perpetually worried man himself.

So he whipped himself into action, got his clerk to dial for him, and thanks to the technology of two complex switchboards a quarter of a mile apart, was eventually connected to a sympathetic, mature and homely female voice that said that she was sorry, she was only a cleaner.

"Was it something that you needed in a hurry, sir? If you'll tell me what it's about, I can have a look on his desk and see if I can find anything."

But then came unexpected progress.

"Are you still there, sir? I don't think he's gone home yet. I think I can hear him in his lav. I'll go and see if I can waylay him for you."

So Hunter and Grimshaw were brought together; but Hunter did not seem to know what Grimshaw was talking about.

"File? I'm sorry. What file was that?"

"This morning—" Grimshaw began to say.

"I'm sorry. We've got a terrible line. Look—can you meet me in ten minutes in the Carders' Arms? I wanted a chat with you, anyway, and some things go down better over a jar."

The Carders' Arms was a pub in a lane behind W. H. Smith's wholesale warehouse. It claimed—along with several others—to have the smallest bar in the kingdom. It was not disputed by the many customers who had been there only once that it had the dirtiest pumps, the most corroded pipes and the worst beer in Bradburn. For this reason it was deserted when Hunter and Grimshaw went in, except for two immigrants who were talking in their own language. Hunter kept his voice low.

"This has been going on for several years. We don't expect you to get a result the first day you've worked on it, you know."

"No—but if you've a file missing, the sooner we move in, the better chance we stand."

Hunter laughed that off with mock horror, not meant unpleasantly.

"Move in? May Heaven forfend: what consternation would that cause in my dove-cotes? I mean, don't think I'm spelling my rights out, Grimshaw, but I haven't invited you to move in yet. Until I do—"

Was this the man who this morning had been so keen to see Councillor Whitcombe get his?

"You and I are friends, I hope, Grimshaw. I can't quite think how we're going to handle this if things don't stay like that."

"Of course things must stay like that."

"And as for a missing file—you can safely leave that to me. It's not entirely unprecedented, in offices the size of ours, for a file to go missing."

No, Grimshaw supposed not.

"As a matter of fact, I know perfectly well where this one is. That bugger Whitcombe has it."

That was more like it.

"Got it unofficially. Corner-cutting. Nothing on the record. Some Registry clerk's going to have to have his knuckles rapped for connivance. But the file will come back. Slipped back where it belongs—or somewhere near to where it belongs. They'll say it was a misfile. But I'll catch the buggers this time. There'll be papers missing from it of course, and we shall never know what they contained. Whitcombe's got it out to weed it. He must be crossing palms, down in Registry. But I'll have them, when they try to slip it back. I'm ready for them, this time."

"Well, I'm always grateful to anyone who saves me work," Grimshaw said, without energy. He was sick to the back teeth even of his own catch-phrases.

"Glad to be of service. No, seriously, Grimshaw, let's

get all the decks clear between us: there'll come a day, and may it be soon, when you'll come in through our main door with warrants. Until then, we mustn't have Whitcombe and his pals scared into inactivity. I've got a feeling that it's their next crime, not their last, that we're going to get them for. Forward planning may be easier to spot than past history. And we are not going to catch them by issuing plain warnings that we're lying in ambush."

"I'm with you all the way, Hunter."

"Good. I didn't think we were going to have serious difficulties. So you'll call your people off?"

"My people are not on."

"Oh, come now! One minute you say we're in full agreement, the next—"

"I'm handling this myself, in close collaboration with my Chief. The reason I wanted to see you again today was to clear everything with you."

"But isn't Inspector Mosley one of yours?"

"Mosley is more than fully occupied with murder and magic in Marldale."

"Mosley was fully occupied this afternoon in the County Offices. He was in the Planning Department asking to see Councillor Whitcombe's secretary."

There were no messages in from Mosley. Mosley had been in County Hall this afternoon, if Hunter said so, but the sly old devil had been nowhere near police headquarters. Just for once, however, there was consolation. Just for once Mosley had so far compromised with contemporary practices as to establish an Incident Room. Grimshaw settled for an evening drive to Marldale.

But first he bought an evening paper: he always liked to inform himself early of public criticism of his Department and his colleagues. Yet tonight he had to search to find the word "police" in print. Even the name of "Crafty Jack" Mosley had not earned a reference. The hideous murder of an isolated old woman, relict of a family once considered influential, appeared to have devolved into a bet about church bells, the deployment of a pack of Alsatians and some obscure—and much-resented—threat to interfere with forthcoming Sheep Dog Trials. Grimshaw pictured the Assistant Chief Constable at home with that newspaper untidily unfolded across the arm of his chair. But this was what the ACC had said he wanted, wasn't it: Mosley in Marldale, diverting attention from County Hall, spraying the horizon with sensational irrelevancies as field-labourers in the old days used to fan out horse-manure? The trouble with the ACC was that he did not always remember what he had said he wanted. And what were the chances, anyway, that Mosley would have Councillor Harry Whitcombe's name in front-page headlines by tomorrow morning?

There was plenty of room for Grimshaw to park in the cold, deserted square of Upper Marldale, though he felt concerned about a gang of juvenile cyclists who were practising wheelies dangerously close to his cherished panels. It did not do for a Detective-Superintendent to drive about looking as if he had been scraped in street traffic.

"Where is the Incident Room?"

"What's an Incident Room?"

"Where's the Community Centre?"

"Over there. But there's nothing on tonight."

Nor was there; that was only too evident. And since no one had the lamp over his front door switched on tonight, Grimshaw had to go over to the door of the Centre to read the roughly lettered card that Mosley had pinned there. Grimshaw tried the door, though all was darkness inside. He hammered on the door; but Dick Hardcastle had gone home to watch snooker on telly.

So what now? Call in at the Crook, in case anyone in there was talking about the murder? No: stay away from the Crook. In case anyone in there was talking about the murder.

Had they not agreed that it was a good thing to leave everything in Mosley's hands? Well—everything was in them.

Grimshaw went home.

Chapter Twenty-one

Mosley and Beamish had another morning drive over the hills to Marldale. They had not met since mid-morning yesterday, when Mosley had despatched the sergeant to Pringle Hospital. "There are one or two things I want to get off my chest," Beamish said, narrowly missing a cat that came from under a milk-float.

"It's always as well to keep your bronchial tubes clear," Mosley said.

"I'm not making jokes about it, sir. You'd no right to saddle me with this rubbish about Marldale church clock."

"I'm sorry, Sergeant. I'd have thought you would have found it fun."

"I'm getting all the fun I want trying to keep my mind on a major murder."

"All murders are major, as far as the murdered person's concerned. I'd have thought you'd have found this other thing a challenge."

"The word *challenge*, Inspector, is the most over-worked lump of bullshit in the English tongue, fit only for use by Chief Constables and politicians."

"I'm glad you've spat that out. Anything else irritating your membranes this morning?"

"Yes. You shouldn't have sent me down to Pringle Hospital yesterday morning. It was no part of my duties. It immobilized me for the rest of the day, as far as any useful work was concerned. And it showed no consideration for the patient. Even now I wouldn't be surprised to hear that he's had a relapse."

Mosley looked concerned.

"You did drop in on the Matron's office first—say that I'd sent you?"

"I did."

"In that case the medical responsibility is entirely theirs."

"Oh, they didn't mind at all. They seemed to welcome me. They seemed to think it was a good thing to exercise his brain."

"So?"

"His brain's too much in need of exercise, for one thing. For another, the stroke affected his speech. He has to struggle to get his words out, and when he does, half of them are in German."

"Do you know any German?"

"A bit."

"Well, then, what are you grumbling about?"

"It upset him terribly, thinking that somebody else was going to bugger about with his clock."

"It isn't his clock. It's the responsibility of the Marldale churchwardens. They may pay him fifteen quid a year to mind it for them."

"I think I got that over to him. I also tried hard to convince him—I think with some measure of success—that I'm a friend of his clock, that I'm the man his clock has been waiting for, that it does a clock no good, standing idle."

"So you found out how how to wind it?"

"Roughly. It's mostly a question of getting weights up with pulleys. But having said that, it also seems to be a clock that knows its own master. There are a ratchet and pawl that stop the movement slipping back while you're raising the weights. But they're so worn out that you have to reach down and hold the claw firm with your left hand while you're winding with your right. Peter Muller didn't seem to think my arms are long enough to manage. He's a great six-foot gangling sod, himself."

Silence, while Beamish eased into the traffic stream on one of Bradburn's outer ring road roundabouts.

"Inspector Mosley, I'm not having anything to do with this clock unless you can prove to my satisfaction that it is an essential part of our strategy in collaring the murderer of Beatrice Cater."

"It's going to be that, right enough, I'm afraid."

"You're afraid? Be more specific."

"In due course."

"I find that a lame answer."

"I can see a skeleton, Beamish. Wait till I find the meat."

Further silence, while Beamish considered whether to commit himself. The truth about Mosley's strategy, surely, was that Priscilla Bladon had to be kept sweet at all costs.

"Anyway, you've already told Priscilla Bladon that you'll do it," Mosley said.

"I haven't. I simply avoided insubordination in public."

"Same thing."

"You're a persuasive old devil. As a matter of fact, I've thought of two possible ways in which it could be managed."

"I knew you had it in you."

"Electric motor, time-switch controlled, to haul up the weights. It will need a cam-operated arm to hold the pawl and ratchet thing steady."

"Well done! The only thing is that the security people will do a thorough search of the tower before they seal it off. So I'm sorry—that's out."

"In that case, get Flavour Control, Ltd. to mix a potion that will distract the dogs."

"Can't allow that, Beamish. It would compromise the ploy they've got on for the Sheep Dog Trials. We mustn't spoil that. It's the one thing that will settle Bert Garside."

"Well—if you think that that filthy footpath is more important than a village playing-field—"

"Bert Garside thinks he is bigger than community rights. That's important, too. It wouldn't work, anyway. The point is that Bert's dog's going to abandon the sheep to chase non-existent bitches. They may be using bitches to guard the tower."

"So what happens when a bitch smells the bitch of bitches?"

"I don't know, and I prefer not to experiment."

"You prefer not to experiment?"

Beamish said the words quietly, incisively, bitterly. But if Mosley saw any irony in them, he did not comment on it.

"And what contribution to criminal detection did you make after you got rid of me?" Beamish asked him.

"I? Oh, I had a day with the innocents."

"And none so innocent as 'Crafty Jack,' I suppose?"

"Sergeant Beamish, it is not the done thing to throw journalistic imbecilities at one's colleagues."

"Sorry."

Which he was. Mosley was capable of being hurt—and even at his most exasperating, one did one's best not to hurt him.

"Really. A day of innocents. You know how it is—or you ought to by now. What is the first gift a good fairy should give a detective at birth? The ability to know whether people are telling the truth or not."

Beamish said nothing. Mosley was skirting round the dirty word intuition, and he did not want to be trapped into agreeing with the old man.

"There's nothing magic about it. No need for witchcraft. I could break it down for you into signs and symptoms, if I didn't think you knew them already. But there's a lot more to it than sweaty palms and shifty eyes. There's a blue-print built up in the bottom of your mind. You apply it to everybody that you talk to. Obviously the more you've got in the bottom of your mind, the more reliance you can put on it."

"They set store by lie-detectors in the States."

"That's when you've got someone else to convince, besides yourself. I didn't need electric terminals and a print-out on graph-paper to know that young Roger Somers is about as straight a dealer from the top of the pack as you'll find on the County payroll. Three A Levels. Young family. Taking professional exams in his own time to advance himself. Everything to lose if he doesn't keep his nose clean."

"Beatrice Cater's young friend—"

"And by God, did he hate the sight of her coming in at his door? What Hindle told us was true: she wasted no time in preliminaries. Offered him earners on her extension plans within a minute of walking into his office. Persistent, too. We know, don't we, that she'd no finesse? In the end he left instructions that he was not available when she called. And you see the corollary of that, I take it?"

"That he has a loyal staff?"

"Oh, come on, Beamish—detect, detect, detect!"

"That she must have called in his office more often than the two occasions that Major Hindle told us about."

"Saved yourself just in time, my lad! And one more rider?"

Beamish thought, but this time did not see what Mosley could be getting at.

"It wasn't Roger Somers that she saw the last time Hindle delivered her to County Hall. Given which, it isn't even certain that she was calling in the Planning Department every time she went there. And that might be important. Because it wasn't in the Planning Department that she was given the desk diary. Somers was stymied by that. He runs a good office, he knows what's in it, and he's one of these men with a photographic memory. He's been in charge for three years and one of the first things he did when he took over was to clear the junk out."

"But a secretary's old desk diary would not be in the general filing system. It might even have been her personal property."

"Somers knew the former secretary: Sally Carver, now an honest married woman, Mrs. Wortham—who left the office four years ago. He knew her well, vouches for her integrity. Also swears that she had left nothing behind her when she resigned, that her desk and cupboards were cleared for her replacement."

"Who might have kept her predecessor's diary for her own guidance."

"She did just that. For a year. We had her in and asked her. She distinctly remembered throwing it away. It had been no use to her—half the entries in it were scrawled abbreviations that she couldn't read. She slung it in her wastepaper basket and never saw it again."

"It could have been rescued by someone else in the office."

"That's a possibility, but I don't know how we'd check it. There's been a fair turnover of juniors in the last four years. Somers is going to put his ear to the ground, but I don't think he'll get anywhere."

"So then you went slumming on the Dales Estate."

"A nice young woman, Beamish. The sort who makes a chap like me conscious of his age, his paunch, his bald patch and the egg on his tie."

"And she's another of your honest types?"

"I've got to say I'm sure of it, Beamish. Another innocent."

"We won't argue about it."

"Bewildered, though. It had been a disturbing experience, being interrogated by Beatrice Cater in hunting mood."

"Being questioned about entries in the diary, you mean?"

"That's right."

"And they were?"

"Two of them were hairdressing appointments. One was to remember somebody's birthday. And two were engagements jotted down for Councillor Harry Whitcombe—so she'd know when the boss was going to be away."

"Interesting?"

"One was an international local government conference at Scheveningen. One was a holiday in Corfu."

"How many people did Mrs. Wortham tell about Mrs. Cater's visit?"

"Her husband."

"And who's he?"

"Top systems man at Pooles in Bradcaster: computer science."

"This is getting rather far away from Beatrice Cater, isn't it? It looks to me as if mares' nests were invented for her special benefit. Is it going to be worth the labour of trying to go into all this?"

"Dare we risk not doing? We might be lucky, Beamish. There's a possible short cut."

"And that is?"

"If we could find who else in Upper Marldale gave her a lift into Bradburn. She's bound to have chattered in the car. She might even have tried to enlist another recruit."

"Or we could put pressure on the coven to tell us what Mrs. Cater really did offer them over the liqueurs."

"Exactly, Beamish. Fancy your chances, pressurizing Priscilla Bladon, do you?"

"Senior man's privilege, I would have thought. I'll have a go at Deirdre Harrison, if you like."

"See what I mean about making the clock chime? That's the only way to the hearts of those three."

A few days ago, Beamish had never set foot in Upper Marldale. Now there was a familiarity that extended even to individual figures standing philosophically on pavement corners. They went into the Community Centre and left the street-door open. Mosley indulged in one of his pensive periods. Beamish was reduced to reading his own notebook.

"Are we waiting for anyone in particular?" he asked.

"Not much point in having an Incident Room if we never man it."

No one came. They waited an hour, at the end of which Hardcastle staggered in with the gallon teapot. Beamish poured two cups, waited till the caretaker had withdrawn to his lair, then took them out and emptied them in the street gutter. Mosley signalled that he had had enough of the Incident Room.

"I've been thinking of something that you volunteered for, Sergeant Beamish. I think it might be quite a good idea."

"What have I let myself in for now?"

"Deirdre Harrison. You might be able to make progress there. Take her out for a meal. Give her a good time."

"If I can find her—"

"What's today? Tuesday? Try the Juvenile Court at Pringle. But you can run me back to Bradburn first. I think it's about time I went and parleyed with Harry Whitcombe."

Chapter Twenty-two

He was tall, appeared to be in his well-preserved seventies—though he must have been younger—and he moved with a slow but ramrod-straight dignity, which accorded with the frightening perfection of his clothes. He gave the impression of being a man who would not deign to wear any garment more than once—not excluding his four hundred pounds' worth of custom-built greatcoat. Moreover, he knew exactly where he was going and had plotted his course in straight lines, even through territory that he had never visited before. One of these courses took him diagonally across the outer office, without reference to the desk, and without deviation up the stairs towards the Chief's room. The Duty Sergeant called him back without effect, made record time over the obstacle course of the counter-flap, caught up with him on the first landing and requested his identity and purpose in life.

"About time too. In the seven seconds that I have been inside this building I have placed four bombs, to say nothing of the havoc I have already wrought in your transport lines and bicycle shed."

The visitor looked at Sergeant Ball down a nose that could have done duty as a ploughshare. Then suddenly he laughed, an orgasm of private mirth produced entirely through that organ, without assistance from any other vocal apparatus. And from somewhere hidden under the lapels of the archducal greatcoat he produced a walleted warrant-card at the sight of which the sergeant all but blenched.

It was seven-thirty in the morning and the visitor had arrived by taxi. Sergeant Ball judged that the only appropriate waiting-room for a caller of such distinction was the

143

Chief's office itself. He alerted the Night Inspector, who was in the wash-room plying his electric razor prior to going off duty. The Inspector crossed his fingers and rang the Chief in bed. The Chief insisted that all his ACCs be brought to their desks immediately. The youngest uniformed constable on the premises was sent upstairs to lay and light the Chief's coal fire, while the visitor, now sitting at the Chief's desk, read without nasal reaction a copy of *Playboy* that he had found in one of the Chief's drawers. The most glamorous woman officer that the Inspector had been able to find in the building knocked and asked if the visitor wanted a cup of tea, to which he said, "No thank you," as if he considered that he had just had a narrow escape.

Grimshaw was at the breakfast-table working his way down the strata of the day's newsprint.

The centre of police interest in the case of the Marldale witches appears to have shifted to Bradburn's exclusive Dales Estate. Urbane Mrs. Sarah Wortham, former Secretary to the Chairman of Bradburn's Planning Committee, declined to comment after a four-hour interview yesterday with Crafty Jack.

Grimshaw closed his eyes. There seemed something remote in the early-morning sounds of his home: other people using the bathroom, the milkman on the doorstep, a blackbird in the garden warning her nestlings of a prowling cat. He opened his eyes again, and the newspaper was still there, its contents unaltered. Then the phone rang.

The Chief was immaculately schooled in the arts of professional conversation. He would not have dreamed of bringing anything of a business nature into the first five minutes of any one-to-one conference.

"Your first visit to Bradburn, sir? Try to find a minute to slip into St. Elfric's. Marvellous angel roof. Try to avoid catching sight of the font, though."

"Two good men you've got here," the Assistant Commissioner (Terrorism) said.

"Glad to hear it. Good lot altogether."

"Your Inspector Bream—"

The Chief had the feeling that it would not be long before he was out of his depth.

"And your Sergeant Moses."

The Chief did not yet connect. He leaned forward across his tooled-leather blotting-pad.

"Perhaps we had better call in my Assistant Chief Constable (Crime). I always believe in keeping subordinates informed of new developments at the earliest possible stage."

"I think we'll keep this *entre nous* for the time being," the AC(T) said.

"As you wish, sir."

"Eighteen months ago an Iranian mole in the Israeli Embassy in Palace Green, Kensington, was found with his throat cut behind a pile of cardboard cartons in Westonbirt Gardens, NW6. A patrol was on the scene within minutes—"

The Chief had just arrived at the thought that it might be Mosley and Beamish that the Assistant Commissioner was talking about. He wondered what they had been doing in London, NW6. He did not remember ever having dealt with the necessary clearance.

"They found incontrovertible evidence that someone had had sexual intercourse in an adjacent carton, also within minutes of the crime. I won't trouble you with how we come to be so certain of the timing. There is no need for me to go into what can be inferred from contraceptive detritus."

"No need whatever," the Chief said.

"It may seem a far cry from a political assassination in North West London to the murder of a South Coast Mayor while he was crowning his annual Rose Queen. You remember the case?"

"Vividly."

"Shot with a sniper's rifle from the steeple of a neighbouring church."

"And no arrest was ever made."

"That is unfortunately so. Though from our point of view we did gain valuable information. What the general public never knew was the reason for a brief and arhythmical tolling of the tenor bell whilst ambulance workers were still comforting the Queen's infant attendants on the platform. Of course, people obsessed by the supernatural were able to come to facile conclusions. But again there was evidence—on which I will forbear to expand—that the same sort of thing had happened in the belfry as had gone on in the cardboard box. The couple must have been leaning against the tenor bell and their climactic excitement would appear to have activated its clapper. Only briefly, as I say. But it is an interesting point, and one which features in a number of subsequent case-histories, that they were prepared to jeopardize their finely timed escape to assuage appetites that many operators would have been content to postpone."

"A passionate pair, I would imagine."

"They must be. It takes a fair output of erotic abandon to agitate a two-ton bell. We tried reconstruction—stopping short, of course, of an actual peal. However, that's beside the point. There have been other instances, mostly political. An Irish publican in Barking, liquidated, we think, by an Ulster faction for allowing his clientele to sing songs deriding the Black and Tans. The retired captain of a Fisheries Protection Vessel, stabbed on an allotment garden in Huddersfield—a revenge killing for something that happened during the Cod War. In some cases the differences settled were essentially private: you remember the electrocution-in-the-lift case?"

"Clearly."

"Managing director of a leading travel firm, obviously obliterated at his wife's instigation. In any number of files we have the same syndrome: extermination by contract, followed at once by procreative fervour. At Huddersfield that act was performed in a henhouse, in full view of a dozen Rhode Island Reds."

"Disgraceful."

"We are up against dangerous people, Chief Constable."

"To tell you the truth," the Chief said, "I have never fully understood how these contracting agents work. How do they tout for custom? Suppose that you or I had someone on the periphery of our lives who was becoming altogether too much for us: how would we set about appointing our proxy? Presumably it would be a question of consulting metaphorical Yellow Pages?"

"We would ask around in the right places. A lot would depend upon whom we knew—and what confidence they had in us."

"I think I see."

"And on our clear ability to pay in spotlessly laundered money. A third of the fee in advance is a conventional token of trustworthiness. Anyway, I am sorry in some ways, glad in others, that your bailiwick has been chosen as the latest theatre of operations. Glad because your Inspector Bream—"

"Sergeant Beamish."

"And your Sergeant Moses—"

"Inspector Mosley."

The Assistant Commissioner (Terrorism) pointed his nose at the Chief Constable the way he had pointed it at Sergeant Ball. He had a metropolitan contempt for these provincials who did not even know the names of their own lieutenants.

"Your two officers—"

"Good men—"

"They are indeed. They have put their fingers in a trice on the key feature that is going to break this case. We have, as you can imagine, questioned many thousands of suspects. Their signed statements occupy many dozens of filing cabinets. But thanks to computerization, our retrieval system can throw up distinguishing marks in a matter of seconds: hair lips, cleft palates, glass eyes and warts under shoulder-blades."

"Wonderful."

"But in only one case have we come across facial scars left by surgery on tubercular glands."

"Ah."

"Which is precisely what your Inspector and sergeant have unearthed in Marldale."

"Application," the Chief Constable said. "The number of times I have preached that word to them—"

"This man—the one with the scars—is undoubtedly

one who helped with enquiries for several days at Huddersfield. Close-run thing. He had particles from a Rhode Island feather caught up in the zip of his flies, but the Yard solicitor took counsel's opinion and it was decided on balance that that evidence was too likely to be dismissed as circumstantial. But this time—"

The AC(T) started to laugh for the second time that morning, the same nasal trumpeting as had alarmed Sergeant Ball. The Chief, not recognizing it as laughter, waited in increasing concern until it was shut off abruptly at source.

"This time we've got him. I have that gut feeling. We shall, of course, be relieving you of your burden of responsibility for the case. Authorization is on its way from the Home Office. I shall be personally in command and I have a comprehensive team already speeding up the motorways. I would like first, please, to see your current working log."

"Ah, yes, gentlemen," Grimshaw said, in the inspiration of crisis. "We believe here in keeping the paper-work down to a minimum, and all the working documentation is in our Incident Room in Upper Marldale."

And the ACC (Crime) said that all the relevant papers were in his Detective-Superintendent's hands; noninterference, when everything was going well, that was always the motto of the ACC. So Grimshaw was brought upstairs, too, much to the Chief's comfort, for in times of confusion and peril he greatly liked to be surrounded by men of good faith who might possibly know what any of it was about.

"Ah, yes, gentlemen," Grimshaw said, in the inspiration of crisis. "We believe here in keeping the paperwork down to a minimum, and all the working documentation is in our Incident Room in Upper Marldale."

"Incident Room. Yes, of course. I shall be taking your Incident Room over. I take it you will run me there presently. But I am a man who believes in taking bulls by horns, and I first wish to call on this Councillor, Whitwell, is it? I would like you to come with me, Grimshaw. As Detective-Superintendent, I take it your finger-tips are on all the sensitive personality pulses."

"Yes, sir. If I might just have five minutes to brief my divisions."

Five minutes in which to despatch a muster-team to Marldale with instructions to make the Community Centre look like the busiest Incident Room in the history of detection. Five minutes also in which to set every other available man and woman in the headquarters on the one task that was to have priority until it had been achieved: find Mosley.

Chapter Twenty-three

The Magistrate's Court in Pringle was held in a grim stone cube of a building whose soulless windows had looked down on a century and a half of melancholy histories. Beamish ran Deirdre Harrison to earth in a dusty little room at the back which was used to isolate witnesses. Ms. Harrison was alone in that room with a stocky, bristle-haired thirteen-year-old, and as Beamish entered her arm was cleaving the air through an arc of a hundred and ten degrees. Her palm connected. The boy lurched to his right and braced his leg to stop himself from falling.

"Right?" she asked him.

"Right, miss."

She turned and caught sight of Beamish, signalled to the lad to make himself scarce.

"You didn't see that, Sergeant."

"It didn't happen," he assured her.

"The little bugger got off," she said.

"I was wondering—"

"Hadn't you better caution me first?"

"I was wondering whether you'd let me take you out to dinner tonight."

She adjusted a shoulder-strap: she was back in bib-and-brace.

"I wouldn't have your job for four times what they pay you, Sergeant. The things you have to go through when duty calls. Where were you thinking of taking me? Smoky Joe's?"

"Your choice."

"That means I'm on expenses."

"You're not."

"Dutch, then. No strings."

"Fair enough. And we'll talk about only what you want to talk about."

"You might live to regret that. There are one or two questions that I'm dying to ask you. Do you know the Peacock at Pringle?"

"No, but I'll find it."

"I hardly think it's the body beautiful you're questing for. Don't tell me I've met a man at last who's spotted my lovely soul."

The Assistant Commissioner's eyes wandered without a great deal of interest over such sights of Bradburn as Grimshaw pointed out. "What can you tell me about this man Whitcombe, Superintendent? I only know what I read about him in this morning's paper."

As Grimshaw had been called to HQ before he had got deeper than the first two in his pile, he did not know as much as that.

"Local businessman," he said. "Very well liked. Started life as a pharmaceutical chemist—dispenser in his father's shop. Since it all came into his hands he's developed it more and more on the lines of an American drug store. He bought adjacent properties and expanded into them. You can buy ironmongery, stationery, gramophone records—and the more the shop has prospered, the less he's had to do with the day-to-day running of it. He's been in local government since they hailed him as the youngest County Councillor in the record books. The local *Examiner* sometimes calls him Mr. Planning. Very popular with the electorate—especially the tradespeople. He has had a very sharp eye for what makes a town prosper."

"The press seem to connect him with the sale of a field in Marldale."

"They've known that from pub talk since Day One, but he'd have served a writ on them in no time, if they'd published his name in connection with the case on supposition. Now that our Inspector Mosley has openly been to talk to his former secretary, they have said whose secretary she was—no more. That's the writing on the wall for anyone in Bradburn."

"I must say that four hours seems a long time for a preliminary interview with a woman in her own home," the AC said.

"I dare say *four hours* is creative writing. Half an hour is probably nearer the mark, knowing Mosley."

"I'm dying to meet your Inspector Mosley."

"So am I," the Detective-Superintendent said.

Five minutes later, Grimshaw had still not caught up with Mosley, but he knew where he had been. It was not that Mosley smoked an exotic tobacco—he combusted a virulent brand favoured by many thousands of fellow addicts. Perhaps there was something about the way he smoked it: in the ten seconds after applying flame to his briar, he invariably produced a screen that some performers would have wished to see accredited in the *Guinness Book of Records*. And there was no doubting that within the last hour, Mosley had surrounded himself with characteristic billows in Councillor Whitcombe's magnificent sitting-room. There were even scrapings of Mosley's vicious dottle in the chromium-plated ashtray beside the chair in which Mosley had sat.

Whitcombe caught Grimshaw's eye just as it lighted on this evidence. Grimshaw and Whitcombe exchanged understanding looks. Whitcombe knew that Grimshaw knew that Mosley had been here. But for some extraordinary reason, Whitcombe did not propose to volunteer this information in his present company. Grimshaw made the silent, crucial decision to play along with him. The conduct of affairs was now entirely in the hands of this long-nosed god from out of the central machine, who knew so little of Mosley that he had only recently succeeded in getting his name right.

And how was the Assistant Commissioner (Terrorism) going to tackle a complex County Councillor of whom he knew no more than he had read in half a line in his morning paper? What excuse was he going to proffer for their even being here? There was a comfort in Councillor Whitcombe's bucket chairs that communicated itself even unto the soul. Grimshaw settled down to learn by observation of the great, the thought not far from his mind that perhaps, after all, he was going to come away from this interview with quietly increased confidence in their local way of setting about things.

"Bit early to offer you anything but coffee," Harry Whitcombe said. "Have you gentlemen any preference? We have Kenyan, Guatemalan, Costa Rican. I think we may be temporarily out of Martinique—"

They came to a largely arbitrary accord.

"So," the Assistant Commissioner (Terrorism) said, "investigations seem to have come round to your former secretary. I must point out that you are not obliged to make any comment—but is there anything you could tell us that you think we ought to know?"

Whitcombe happily waved aside the need for the conventional caution.

"Only that, of course, my former secretary—as you call her—is only on the extreme periphery of recent unhappy events. She has twice received visits in circumstances which any woman must find frightening—in the first place by the woman whose murder has brought you to these parts."

"And what was the purpose of that visit?"

"Mrs. Cater had by some means come by an old desk diary that Sally Wortham used to keep in her secretarial days."

"And what was her interest in that diary? Blackmail?"

"No. She was asking for clarification of a number of entries which could mean nothing at all to any outside reader."

"Can you be more explicit about these entries?"

"Yes. I can tell you about them. They refer to two overseas visits which I made four years ago."

"Would you like to go into detail?"

"Yes. I will tell you everything. The first was to Scheveningen, where a composite working-party of EEC elected representatives and specialist officials had been convened to produce a paper on common policies in the planning field."

"Why should that interest Mrs. Cater?"

"Because my most vivid memory of Scheveningen was of another Englishman—his name was Hilgay—who was a private guest in the same hotel. Hilgay went to quite sick-

eningly obvious lengths to get to know me, to importune
me in the bar between our official sessions, to buy me
drinks—and with considerable skill try to extract information about future development projects in this county."

"And you know other things about this Hilgay?"

"Very little. An occasional entrepreneur, that's the only
way I can think of describing him, because he is not a known
name in the world of developers. I had all but forgotten
him until some months after my return home. Then he
turned up as the spokesman of a small syndicate that wanted
to buy some relatively waste land as a grouse moor. They
got it, because their offer was viable and we had no use for
the land in the thinkable future: it had been bought as an
investment in the Railway Age. What I did not know at the
time—Tweedledum and Tweedledee are not always aware
what each other has in mind—was that the General Post
Office was considering a requisition order on that land for
an internal communications station. Hilgay and his friends
cleared up a profit which would have been welcomed by
the County Treasurer."

"But none of this would be in Mrs. Wortham's diary,
surely?"

"No. But it is interesting that on a date six weeks before
I went to Scheveningen, she had scribbled in Hilgay's name,
alongside a telephone number."

"Not at your instigation?"

"Certainly not."

"At whose, then? Hilgay's?"

"I think that will become apparent. May I go on with
my second instance?"

"Please do."

"It was in Corfu, in the early autumn of that year,
where I went to holiday with my wife, and once again found
an English guest who was a pain in the neck. This one was
quite candidly looking for a profitable deal in premises in
which he could establish a private nursing home."

"And he eventually found his way to one, I suppose?"

"The Evenlode, on the outskirts of this town. And I
assure you, Assistant Commissioner, the transaction was
constitutional down to the last half-line of small print."

Coldly professional, the AC(T) avoided any remark. "And there was a diary entry about this?"

"The name of this Englishman—Barnes—was pencilled in in brackets after the word *Corfu* on the date of my departure."

"You seem very well informed indeed about the conversation between Mrs. Cater and Mrs. Wortham."

"Well, naturally I am. Mrs. Wortham was extremely worried by the woman's visit. She rang me to ask me for my advice. I forced her to remember every question that Mrs. Cater had asked her."

"You have remained close to Mrs. Wortham since her retirement?"

"Far from it. I don't think I have set eyes on her more than twice in four years. But you see she did consider herself my secretary—"

"Consider herself? That is twice, Councillor Whitcombe, that you have attempted to qualify her position as secretary—"

"Because she was not *my* secretary, in the sense that she was never my employee. Please understand, I always found her extremely agreeable and efficient down to the final comma. But she was the servant of the County Council, and her job was in theory secretarial to whoever happened to be in the Chair of the Planning Committee. It is coincidental that I have held that honour for many years now."

"I see. So her ultimate master would be the Head of the Personnel Department—?"

"Ultimately the Chief Executive Officer, a man whom we all know as Tod Hunter. And when Mrs. Wortham rang me, both after Mrs. Cater's visit, and yesterday after Inspector Mosley's, it was to the CEO that I referred her. I'm sure you will admit that that was the logical step for me to take."

Grimshaw managed to look Whitcombe full in the face. A mention of Mosley: so was Whitcombe now going to admit that Mosley had already heard all this from him this morning?

No. Whitcombe looked away again. But was it Grimshaw's imagination, or had a faint smile played across his lips?

The Assistant Commissioner looked at his watch.

"Well, this is all very interesting, Councillor, and there are a good many points which I shall want to follow up. But at the moment I must be elsewhere. I will be inviting you to come and talk to me at headquarters."

"No," Harry Whitcombe said with unruffled firmness.

"You would not wish to put yourself in an invidious position, I am sure."

"If you arrest me, and if I am to be immediately charged with some offence, I shall, of course, not resist. But I do not propose to become the object of speculation by being seen accompanied to a place where you cannot compel me to come. Moreover, I am adult enough to know what is going on in your mind, Assistant Commissioner, and I shall not voluntarily put you in a position to play psychological games with me. You are welcome to come here and talk at any time of night or day."

Greek and Greek? The Assistant Commissioner took aim with his formidable nose—and Councillor Whitcombe was proof against it. Now there was no doubt that he was faintly smiling.

"And if I were you two gentlemen, I'd save myself a lot of trouble, and go and talk to your Inspector John Mosley. He's miles ahead of you about all this—miles ahead."

Grimshaw also stole a look at his watch and wondered what progress, if any, his shock troops had made in the establishment of at least the external appearances of an Incident Room. Was there even a telephone on the premises?

"This Chief Executive Officer, Grimshaw—?" the AC(T) asked, as they climbed the first of the hills out of Bradburn.

"A man of transparent integrity," Grimshaw said.

"They invariably are."

"Family man, ordinarily dressed, modest home, kids at the neighbourhood school, sand-castles and beach cricket for their summer holidays."

"Sounds like the perfect cover to me."

"I'm not going to stick my neck out, sir. But I shall be interested in your reactions when you come to meet him."

"I once arrested a man, Grimshaw, who had thrown a bomb into a school playground, killing four infants and a teacher, grievously maiming a dozen others. All because a supergrass had two children on the roll. And yet, you know, we had it on good report that only the previous week this chappy had seen a blind old woman across a road. Tell me more about Hunter."

"Boot-strapped himself up from virtually nothing through professional qualifications covering diverse fields."

"Must be pretty proud of himself."

"I think he's entitled to be. But he's certainly not ostentatious about it."

"Stashing away for early retirement, you think?"

"I do know he's always saved furiously for the time when his children's education's going to come expensive."

"That sort of saving can become obsessive."

"A lot of people do it."

"And some people are in a stronger position than others to pull off the occasional big one. It can be habit-forming. And a self-made man falling from a high position sometimes takes it very badly. It's more than he can face."

"Don't think I'm trying to be his advocate, sir. I hope I've held my present post long enough to be beyond surprises. I find it difficult to picture Tod Hunter even knowing where to start looking for a contract killer."

"Surely the CEO of an organization as big as a County Council has to know whom to contact for anything on earth?"

"Anything legal."

"Oh, come, Grimshaw. You know as well as I do that half the dignitaries at any civil reception ought to be under lock and key."

"I've been heard to say those very words," Grimshaw said.

They turned into the *Narrow Road with Passing Places* which half the sheep on the Pennines seemed to prefer to the grazing on either side of it. Grimshaw wondered if it would have occurred to anyone that a commendable preliminary move would be to sweep the floor of the Community Centre.

Beamish lingered in the precincts of the Pringle Juvenile Court for half an hour longer than honest duty called for. Deirdre Harrison went and fetched two cups of coffee from some contact she had with the permanent denizens of the building. It was lukewarm and coffee-coloured—and was what Beamish imagined that brew had been like which Nazi Occupied Europe had infused for itself from ground acorns.

PC Sid Bowman happened to be waiting to give evidence in a case of theft of a brassière from a clothes-line and it was he who took a telephone call which caused him to break up the interlude in the ante-room.

"Beamish here. Yes: I can make it in less than twenty minutes—yes, I quite see that we had better pull out the stops. Certainly, Mr. Mosley."

Grimshaw was beginning to believe that life in Upper Marldale whenever he arrived there was a closely scripted scene from some over-rehearsed workshop drama in which no actor was ever allowed to vary his movement from one performance to another. The same women were congregated outside the supermarket with the same packets of convenience food protruding from their plastic shopping-bags. The same cyclist had reached precisely the same spot on Market Hill with his rabbit-hutch. But today there were differences. So many police vehicles were parked outside the Community Centre that it was likely to be the general public who brought charges of obstruction. Two large yellow British Telecom vans were half on the pavement.

Grimshaw ushered the Assistant Commissioner through the main door to find a row of half a dozen trestle-tables dressed in line along either side of the hall. At each of these an officer in mufti was poring over sheaves of paper in issue filing-trays. At the far end, sitting on the platform at a table with his homburg on it, Mosley, like a macabre minor princeling holding court, had obviously just applied fire to his pipe.

"Making progress with getting the phone on, I take it?" Grimshaw asked him.

"Actually, no. Some delay in the paper work. But the engineers happened to be repairing the kiosk in the Square, so I asked them to park outside here. I thought it might help us to look willing."

Chapter Twenty-four

A few weeks before his secondment to Marldale, Beamish had done an infiltration job for which he had had to cultivate an appearance: a close-cropped green wig, though he had baulked at the cockades that some of his temporary associates sported; a loosely hanging patchwork cloak that would have offended the brethren of Joseph; and gumboots.

He thought it might put Deirdre more at her ease if he reverted to this rig for their evening out, though he omitted one or two accessories: the safety pin in one ear and the stud in one nostril. It was unfortunate that Deirdre had also departed from her norms, wishing Beamish to see her feminine potential. Since the evenings were chilly, a summer dress seemed inadvisable, and the wisdom of this decision was reinforced when she discovered how much amorphous girth she had acquired since last she had worn one. So she had put on a maroon frock in velvety material that she had last shown to the public three years ago, at a finical old crone's charity bun feast. It seemed now to hang where it should be clinging, and clung where it ought to have hung. But this was as nothing compared with her horror at its pointed lace collar, which made her feel like an addition to the Brontë brood. The collar had to be rapidly unpicked; and when she saw the discolouration underneath it, it had to be sewn on again, which almost made her late for the date. They met on a corner of Pringle Market Place—and each stood and laughed at the sight of the other's strategy.

"They'll never let you into the Peacock," Deirdre said.

"And I wouldn't give much for your chances in Smoky Joe's."

They compromised with a motel restaurant on the Bradcaster by-pass, where they were relatively insensitive to fashion.

"So," she said. "We have a visitor from Olympus. What's the verdict?"

"I've only seen him at a distance. I hope I shall be able to keep that distance. He doesn't look as if he'll have much sympathy with witchcraft."

"I'm wanting out of that, anyway. Sue Bexwell feels the same, and I think Pris Bladon would give her ears for an honourable escape route."

"You've had fun."

"We'd have some more—if there was a cat in hell's chance of winning the playing-field. But there's no way we can cope with that clock on the *Herald*'s terms."

"You know that Mosley has ordered me to see that you win the bet?"

"Not seriously?"

"Mosley was serious."

"So you've got a plan?"

"Several. But we can't beat this Army Corps that the big man from London has brought with him. There'll be no space for manoeuvre in the churchyard."

"It'll take more than a gramophone record of Saint-Saëns this time. I'm afraid the playing-field's a lost cause. And who are the pincers closing in on? Am I allowed to ask?"

Almost every shred in Beamish's make-up was for loyalty to Official Secrets. But he saw a slim chance.

"One leak deserves another."

"What do you want to know?"

"Why you three didn't buy what Mrs. Cater knew."

"The price was unacceptable."

"And the price was?"

"We were to drop the playground idea. Suddaby's field was for a hostel for the Glasshouse inmates."

Then before Beamish could give away any operational confidences he felt a presence behind his chair. He turned and saw a young man of a type with whom he had become familiar during his infiltration exercise: a ritual hair-style attributed to American Indians. And he had with him a girl who was doing her best to emulate him, but was defeated by her peakiness. She looked too young, too unfilled-out to be sleeping away from home in NCOs' old cubby-holes.

Deirdre introduced them: Merle Cox and Kevin Kenyon.

"Miss—they're here again—they're staying in the annexe."

"Who are here again? Take your time, Kevin."

"Those three who stayed in the Glasshouse. But they're different. You wouldn't think they were the same people. But that one, the one with the scars—I'd know him anywhere."

"Are you sure, Kevin?"

Beamish was in no doubt. It was true because it was expected. And if they were here, it could mean only one thing: that they believed—because either Harry Whitcombe or Tod Hunter believed—that when the witches had come away from the Old Tollhouse, Beatrice Cater had told them what she knew.

"Where are they now?"

"They've gone into the bar."

"OK," Deirdre said. "Leave them to us. Don't let them see you staring at them, and don't speak to us again. Don't even look as if you know us. Go on, now—scatter!"

The three people were already coming into the main dining-room, looking for a waitress to show them to a table: two men and a woman. Deirdre was in the better position to see them.

"My God—I hope I never come up against them!"

"Let's hope you don't."

"The one with the scars is bad enough—but his mate—! I've not believed in original sin since I rumbled Father Christmas—but I'd have to revise my theology if I saw much of that one."

"And the woman?"

"Hard—and soft. Cruel eyes and a weak mouth. Straight on to the bed after watching a woman's neck snap! She looks the part."

"Deirdre, I'm sorry to break this up. I'll finish my

meal, because they mustn't see I'm in a hurry. But we mustn't hang about longer than we need. I have things to do."

"Of course you have. There's always the day after tomorrow. Dress for the Peacock next time! And why not leave me here to keep an eye on them?"

"Because you're one of three on their hit list."

Only when their coffee was served in the lounge was Beamish able to get a useful view of the trio. The men could have passed themselves off as executive types, or salesmen for computer software. After all, why should not an exclusive sales rep have eyes that would smile only at the sight of the ultimate fear on a victim's face? And as for the woman, the last time Beamish had seen her like had been in a French film with captions: mostly shot through the louvres of a flat over a village *patisserie*.

It was impossible to use the pay-phone of the motel, which was sheltered only by an acoustic hood. It seemed a long drive before they found a booth from which Beamish could raise HQ, and then, since the AC's staff were now manning their own switchboard, he was dealing with strangers. The Duty Inspector was the highest up the ladder that he could reach, and he was so unexcited by the news that it seemed doubtful whether he was going to take it seriously.

"I'd better follow this up every inch myself," Beamish told Deirdre. "The first step, as always, is to look for Mosley."

Among his follow-up force, the AC(T) had brought a Chief Inspector from the Fraud Squad and it was with this gentleman (who looked more like an escapee from a heavy mob) that he went to call on Tod Hunter, suavely and apologetically telling Grimshaw that he thought three would be too many for the interview. Grimshaw nailed Mosley down and took him with him to see Mrs. Wortham—because he fancied that there was a lot about the former secretary that so far only Mosley knew.

"We are sorry to intrude yet again, Mrs. Wortham, but there are one or two things I'm not clear about."

Mosley sat balancing his homburg upside down on his knee and looked as if his apology for Grimshaw's intrusion was genuine.

"I'm not quite sure of the machinery, Mrs. Wortham, by which a secretary at County Hall is expected to serve two masters."

"I was never aware of any conflict," she said.

"I'm not suggesting that it ever came to conflict. But when, for example, you wrote the name Barnes in the diary, on the day of Councillor Whitcombe's departure for Corfu, who had told you to do so? Councillor Whitcombe—or Mr. Hunter?"

"It was a reminder to myself."

"I understand that. But from whom did you first hear the name Barnes?"

She had to think about that one. And Grimshaw thought that her difficulty was not remembering the truth, but deciding whether to tell it.

"From Mr. Hunter," she said. "Don't think I'm suffering from delusions of grandeur, Superintendent, but we Chairmen's secretaries were a little more than shorthand-typists. Up to a point, it was our job to try to keep the elected representatives on the rails."

"You mean you had to keep your Chairman on the Chief Executive Officer's rails?"

"That's a misleading way of putting it. It was more a question of administrative consistency. We couldn't, of course, tell our Chairmen what to do; but we could remind them what needed doing. We could shift papers up towards the tops of their in-trays when they had been hanging fire too long."

"So you would get regular memoranda from Mr. Hunter, telling you when to jolly Councillor Whitcombe along?"

"That was more or less how things worked."

"And did you have to jolly him along about Mr. Barnes?"

Again the pause: because she knew that what she was about to say next was another point of no return.

"Councillor Whitcombe had not heard of Mr. Barnes —or of the Mr. Hilgay whom he met in Scheveningen. In both cases, Mr. Hunter had asked me to contact the gentleman concerned and let him know Mr. Whitcombe's dates and travel times."

"So you knew in advance that Councillor Whitcombe was going to meet them—but he didn't?"

She held her lips pursed, which was almost answer enough, because she knew that the truth about this must give everything away. But she had no intention of telling anything but truth: she knew things had reached that point.

"So I suggest, Mrs. Wortham, that Mr. Hunter had specifically told you not to mention Mr. Hilgay or Mr. Barnes to your Chairman."

"He may have done. It is a long time ago."

"He may have done? You mean that he did sometimes give you that kind of instruction?"

"Sometimes."

"And in the cases of Mr. Hilgay and Mr. Barnes?"

"He told me to say nothing to Councillor Whitcombe."

"Did you never ask yourself what it was all about?"

"There were times when it paid not to bother your head. Just to get on."

"Why not bother your head?"

"One didn't want to get involved in intrigues."

"Was life in County Hall as frightening as that?"

"Not frightening, Superintendent. We are not talking about criminal activities—at least, I'm not. You used the phrase *jollying along* just now. There was a tremendous amount of that going on. It was going on all the time. It was the only way the machine ever kept working."

"Mrs. Wortham, we started off by talking about conflict. If there had been a conflict—if you had had to make a loyalty decision—to whom would you have been loyal?"

"That's not a fair question, Mr. Grimshaw."

"Just treat it as a hypothetical one."

"The question never arose—and if it had, I think I would have resigned, rather than risk falling out with either of two men with whom I got on excellently."

"But if it had come to the crunch?"

"If it had come to the crunch, naturally I would have stuck by Mr. Hunter. Mr. Hunter was the permanent head of the administration. Councillor Whitcombe could have vanished the day after any election."

Grimshaw and Mosley walked at a leisurely pace back to Grimshaw's car.

"An innocent party," Grimshaw said. "Hunter would have kept her that way, and that's how she preferred it. Negative knowledge—but it's progress."

"I made as much progress as that when I came to see her yesterday," Mosley said.

Did you ever give this woman a lift into or out of Bradburn?

The Assistant Commissioner's task force was pushing questionnaires on the grand scale. And they unearthed someone who had twice given Beatrice Cater a ride: a milkman, Ernest Hurst, Pringle Model Dairies.

"What—on your float?"

"Friday afternoons I sometimes come round in the car. Bad debts. Special visit looks more impressive. Then I go off to Bradburn to do a bit of shopping for the wife."

"Do you know where Mrs. Cater was going to in Bradburn?"

"The County Offices."

"Did she talk at all?"

"Did she ever bloody stop?"

"So she may have dropped hints about why she wanted to go to County Hall?"

"Dropped hints? My head was bloody rattling with them."

"So you were able to draw conclusions about what her business had been?"

"Able to draw the conclusion that she must be three parts round the twist. Couldn't make head or tail of it, the way she kept jumping from one thing to another. I know it had to do with cleaning women: because the cleaning women draw their pay on Friday afternoons. There was a char she wanted to see about something or other."

"You don't happen to know which department?"

"Yes: Highways. I know that, because I wasted time enough helping her to find it."

* * *

"Actually, it's Mr. Mosley that I wanted to see. You don't know when he's likely to be back?"

"I'm afraid not. But I'd be glad to take a message."

"Happen he's in Pringle or Bradburn. I'll drop by later on. I've got to come back this way."

It seemed important to Beamish to hang on to this man. There was something nervous about him—the sort who came along duty-bound to make a statement, and then if something went wrong in the handling of him, was off into the wilds without ever making it. Not a totally uneducated man: marked regional speech, but well under control; sober suit, not new, but well pressed; a man in his fifties, not corpulent, but did not neglect a healthy appetite; hill-weathered, but not a bumpkin by a long chalk.

"It will keep," the man said.

"Well, perhaps you'll let me have your name and address, and I'll ask Mr. Mosley to call on you. Ah, no—wait—"

Beamish saw Mosley crossing the road to the Incident Room.

"Nah, Bob."

"Nah, Jack."

"Long time no see, Bob."

Bob Mercer, Insurance; knew the way to as many farmhouses and cottages as Mosley did, but had had an inside job for the last few years.

"If we could have a bit of a word, Jack."

"Aye."

And Mercer looked meaningfully towards Beamish. Beamish did not expect Mosley to humour him, but Mosley did.

"You'd better come into the inner office, Bob."

Which meant the crumby little kitchen in which Hardcastle and various women's organizations made tea for which they could have found a use in a tanyard.

"Trouble, Bob?"

"I'm worried, Jack. And I've no right to be telling you this. I've no right to be here. I could get the push if it got out that I'd been—talking about a customer's business, at that. Young Tod Hunter."

"What's he been up to?"

"It's what he's going to get up to that's gnawing at me. I've got one of those feelings about it. Too much said in one breath, if you see what I mean."

"I will if you tell me."

"He rang me, would I go round to his office. Wanted to take out a new life policy. Hell of a big one. £45,000— that's the sort of soft canvass we dream of. But it was as if it was all on the spur of the moment. He wanted it all done straight away. Of course, I told him that at his age and for that sort of sum, it would have to be subject to medical. Well, how soon could that be arranged? He tried to make a joke of it: I'd better get on with this before he changed his mind, the premiums being what I'd just quoted. But that isn't all, Jack. He wasn't himself. He was strung up about something. He asked too many suggestive questions. How soon would the policy be in force? How soon would he be covered? What if he fell under a bus tomorrow? What if he crashed his car? Oh, all said as if it was a joke—and it's not the kind of joke I'm hearing for the first time. But there was something about it that I didn't like, something not as it should be."

"I always keep a weather eye open for things that are not as they should be," Mosley said.

"Well, there you have it Jack, for what it's worth. For God's sake never breathe a word in our office that I've been to see you. But I have. I've got it off my mind. I'll leave you to make what you can of it."

Have you ever seen this woman in any of the offices or corridors of County Hall?

Mrs. Daisy Schofield, office cleaner, of 18, Chapel Brow, came forward. Mrs. Schofield had been plaguing herself for days, had been losing sleep for nights, eaten through and through by the knowledge that she ought to come forward. She knew she had done wrong. But it had been an old diary, hadn't it? It had been thrown away. She had found it in a wastepaper basket, years ago. It had been the picture on the front cover that had attracted her—such a lovely woman, such an honest face, such appealing eyes. (Actually it was one of Manet's prostitutes.)

Daisy Schofield had been feeling fed up, the day she had overheard a conversation between Mrs. Cater and Mr. Somers in the Planning Office: fed up because they were shifting her to Highways next week—after seven years in Planning; fed up because her husband had gone on short time, and their Sandra's marriage was on the rocks. She had heard Corfu mentioned, and that other place, that she did not know how to pronounce. But she recognized both place names. She had read them in the diary. And she knew that Mrs. Cater was being short-changed in her quest for information, knew that they were all a pack of double-dealers, knew that what went on on those trips abroad was to nobody's advantage except those who went.

So she buttonholed Mrs. Cater.

"Excuse me, dearie. I couldn't help hearing what you was talking about in there. I've got something at home that might interest you."

She had made arrangements to meet Mrs. Cater in Highways, but the first time Mrs. Cater had not turned up, and the second time Mrs. Schofield had forgotten to bring the diary. But it had changed hands at last. Maybe somebody was going to be taught a lesson this time. Mrs. Cater had the look of someone who stuck at things once she'd started them.

"What's going to happen to me now, sir?"

The Chief was not in genial mood. He had a detached attitude to crime. Although it was his bread and butter, crime rarely penetrated into his upstairs office except on paper. But crime in the ranks of men like Harry Whitcombe and Tod Hunter distressed him. It was not only the thought that they were letting the Establishment down: it was a tremor in the very joists of the Establishment itself.

"I can see how Harry Whitcombe's got himself into this position," the Assistant Chief Constable said. "You know Harry as well as I do—a Bradburn Patriot, one might almost call him a Bradburn Nationalist. Transport him to a resort as far away from home as the Dutch coast and he's pining for the curlew in the heather. Let him meet somebody in a bar in the Aegean who mentions Marldale Nab and he's having to fight back his sentimental tears. And it isn't that Harry talks big: damn it, as far as the architecture and land usage of Marldale and Pringle are concerned, he *is* big—however casual he may make himself look. But Harry's downfall has been the same as the thing that raised him up: the desire to please everybody about him. Not to impress them, not to recruit them to his side, not to do deals with them to their mutual advantage—to please them, to be the chap they're glad they've met. "I've got friends who'd put good money into a shoot on Pringle Moorside," somebody says to him in a bar in Scheveningen. And Harry knows that it's land that the Council no longer wants. He doesn't know what the Post Office have got on their drawing-board."

"But Tod Hunter does."

" 'Drop in and see me when we get back home,' Harry says. And once Harry has implied a promise, he'll see it through."

"As long as he believes it's legal."

"Oh, Harry wouldn't take chances with the law if he knew he was taking them. He's too keen to stay up on his mountain. But he was beginning to wonder. That to my mind is the biggest surprise that's come out of this so far: that it was Harry who went to Tod as Chief Executive and insisted on his sending three case-histories to his friend in the DPP's office. Because Harry was beginning to suspect, and he wanted to know. He was beginning to suspect Tod—and he had guts enough to let Tod know that. But Tod has enough know-how to submit flawed files to his friend, essential evidence missing. Tod could still bluff things out at that stage."

"This unsigned-for file that they've found in Harry's possession—"

"He's been open enough about that, the AC(T) says. He's often cut red tape with the clerks in Registry. They're always glad enough down there if someone offers to save them work. Something he wanted to look at in his own time, at his own pace."

"So Harry's in the clear?"

"I've had a word with that Chief Inspector they've brought up from Fraud—the one who looks like a gorilla. Nice fellow, though, and knows his stuff. And he says as far as he's concerned there's nothing to go forward against Harry."

"Alas, not true of Tod," the Chief said, and his pity was genuine. "Though they haven't charged him yet. Why is it hanging fire?"

"Some tactic of the Assistant Commissioner. Terrorism is his line, not corruption. It's only a matter of time."

"They'll hit Tod hard."

"Oh, he'll go down. And he all but got away with it. He's always played it as safe as it could be played. A different front man for every transaction, never one professionally known: a man in Hunter's position is always meeting punters who are looking for ways of trebling their capital. Hunter sells introductions, splits the earners."

"But to commission murder—" the Chief said, sincerely dismal that such a path could be trodden by anyone that he personally knew.

"When it comes to men who would contemplate murder, we won't find the answer in your mind and mine. At least, I hope not. But think what Hunter knew he had to lose: job, pension, security, repute. Oh, I know it's the same for any man who gets his deserts in a position like Hunter's. But we've got to take Hunter's own peculiar temperament into account as well: a quiet sort of pride, but a positive one. He came from nowhere and he's ended up by running us all. He has dictated to professionals and democrats for years. He has pontificated. His word has been binding. He might look like a man who has no enemies— but that's only because he defeated them all back along the line. There are plenty waiting to gloat. Oh, no, Chief—I can see how Hunter's mind set him looking for someone to carry out a contract on Mrs. Cater. There were some things that he couldn't face—just could not face."

Beamish knew now on which extension he could get hold of Deirdre Harrison before she set out on her day's differentiation between true deprivation and mere guile.

"Hi!"

"Hi!"

"There's something Mosley has asked me to find out. He seems to think it's top priority."

"I'll try."

"The cat. Mrs. Cater's cat. Boudicca. When you came away that night, after drinking chartreuse, did Mrs. Bexwell anoint the threshold with that essence of lioness she'd had from her husband?"

"She did, yes. Freshening the place up, she called it. Might as well leave a reminder that we were still a power in the land, that was her reasoning."

"Good. That's what Mosley thought. He also wants to know—"

"Thinking big, these days, isn't he?"

"He also wants to know, was Boudicca indoors or out when you came away?"

"Indoors, of course. She wouldn't go through a barrier like that. It was a fresh concentration. It would have turned back a menagerie on heat."

"But she did go through it. The milkman found her outside, couldn't get her to go back."

"My mind reels. This is epoch-making."

"Mosley seems to think so."

Chapter Twenty-five

The Assistant Commissioner (Terrorism) was being criticized in some circles for his apparent hesitation to charge Tod Hunter. Mosley claimed to understand his thinking.

"It's obvious, I'd have thought. Once Hunter's in the slammer, the heavy mob know they can say goodbye to the balance of their fee. They're taking a bigger chance than they care for, as it is. And the AC is waiting until people have congregated for the ringing of the bells before he pounces."

"Oh, that's obviously his chosen battle-ground," the Assistant Chief Constable (Crime) said. "And if I'd known what demands he was going to make on my resources, I'd have launched a special recruiting campaign two years ago."

It was true that the AC(T) had approached the show-down in the spirit of Alamein or Normandy. He had put shadows on the witches that were more like mobile cordons—even on Deirdre Harrison's daily shuttle-service through the webs of neglect, bureaucratic incompassion and domestic ineptitude. He had requisitioned phalanxes from as far afield as Tameside to man the hills against the cohorts that the *Morning Herald* had whipped up to come in and witness either a miracle or a farce.

The Assistant Commissioner had cold contempt for both journalism and witchcraft. The three women were bait for his terrorists; he had no other interest in them. Naturally, he was not setting them up to be shot at. They were to be kept together and closely guarded in Priscilla Bladon's house.

"That's your job, Inspector Mosley—you and Sergeant Bream. I'm not suggesting that you can control them—but you do seem to be able to exercise some vestige of influence over them."

173

He had set up a bell tent in the churchyard, equipped with all sorts of technological visual and acoustic aids. Silhouettes of mobile effigies with pointed hats were going to be seen bobbing about on the canvas, to the accompaniment of witch music recorded by synthesizers. The *Herald*, its adjudicators, its hired security force and its dogs were to be allowed to mount what guard they wanted on the tower, their back-seat co-operation rewarded by a front seat for their camerman if, as was hoped, the silhouettes were sniped at.

"We've no case that will stand up against these three unless we can catch them with murder weapons in their hands."

The assassins had been under consummate surveillance since Beamish had reported their presence: round the clock and with triple back-up. They were known to the motel register as Reginald Bates, Sarah Saunders and Des Stonham: the names barely interested the AC(T)—these three had worn as many labels in their time as they had done jobs. In the daytime, they came and went about Bradcaster like people dedicated to the education of small firms in the potential of electronic office equipment. The Assistant Commissioner had played no small part in shaping the phraseology of the *Morning Herald*, making sure that Bates, Saunders and Stonham were kept informed down to the last detail of the best time and place for them to strike.

The AC(T) had also exercised a seam of imagination that had surprised some of his senior associates. About twenty yards from the tent, and with a footpath trodden towards it so that it could not be missed, he had had a depression stamped out in the ground, even a half-bale of straw scattered about, as if the spot were the regular resort of some-one like Merle Cox and Kevin Kenyon. His argument was that if his strike-force missed the trio in the first round, they might head for a ready-made love-nest for their usual work-out.

"If we don't catch them at one of their specialisms, we'll have them at the other."

Zero hour was from eleven o'clock onwards: even the AC(T) did not need to be persuaded of the mystic significance of midnight. Deployment of the outer defences was completed by first dark and it was at half past eight that the first incident was logged. A detachment borrowed from Bradcaster was straddling Herbert Garside's mud-track, and not all of them had yet settled down to take the exercise seriously. But a hypothetical situation became a reality when two of them heard the time-honoured sounds of someone trying to get through their sector with stealth: the sibilance of long wet grass against clothing—even as careless an indication as a cough.

Immediately, operational cynicism evaporated. The pair who had first heard the would-be infiltrator separated and came down on him from obliquely behind, bringing him down with a classical tackle. His resistance was feeble. He was a frail and elderly man in soaked pyjamas and a cheap towelling dressing-gown who had discharged himself from Pringle Hospital—where the *Morning Herald* was as popular as any newspaper in the wards, and where bets were being taken on the Marldale witches. He had difficulty with his speech, said that his name was Peter Muller, that the church clock was his "dove," and that he was not going to have any police sergeant messing about with it. He was taken at once to operational headquarters.

Yesterday Mosley had actually come into HQ with the express purpose of speaking to Grimshaw. He had an accumulation of rest days owing to him, he told the Superintendent. He knew that the final briefing for tomorrow night's encounter was scheduled for four in the afternoon, and he did not propose to be a minute late for that. But he wished to take the morning off. Grimshaw was uneasy: it was unusual for Mosley to worry over-much about rest days. When he did take one, it sometimes appeared afterwards that he had achieved more in it than he did on a normal working day. Rest days were all too often his opportunity for moving beyond the geographical limits of his proper area. Grimshaw always heard with trepidation that Mosley was ostensibly resting. On the other hand—

"You are up to something, Mosley."

"Private business," Mosley said.

* * *

Beamish was not asked whether they owed him a rest day. Grimshaw did not propose to waste the sergeant's temporary attachment to the Bradburn office, and found him several unfinished case-histories to apply himself to. This made it difficult for him to attend to one or two un-publicized odd jobs that Mosley had deputed to him, but once he was away from HQ, he settled his own priorities. He had to go and see Major Hindle, for example, to find out from him, discreetly but categorically, by what route he had walked to and from the Old Tollhouse on his obliging visits to Mrs. Cater. And Mosley had told him that he could ring up Deirdre Harrison about anything he liked.

Mosley got up early to begin his day of rest and went first to Pringle, to call in the offices of Flavour Controls, Ltd., where he asked for the favour of a little of their chief research chemist's time.

"I need something in a hurry that would be irresistible to a lap-dog," Mosley said.

"A lap?" Bexwell suggested.

"Something that would over-ride any other consider-ation in the creature's mind."

Bexwell looked at Mosley through narrowed eyes.

"Are you trying to get us under the Noxious Substances Act?"

"I have no reason to suppose—"

"We have an organic compound, which has passed its clinical trials, and which we had hoped to market as a means of persuading lost animals to return home. We have how-ever run into snags. Our solicitors have warned us that unscrupulous lonely ladies might use the tincture to teach their pets to find hyper-sensitive zones. Obviously we do not wish to be sued for unforeseen consequences—"

"I am not a lonely lady," Mosley said. "There is no danger that you will corrupt or deprave me. I take it you could supply me with a working quantity in double, possibly treble strength?"

"A working quantity? That depends on what work you have in mind."

But Mosley was not to be drawn on that—and was persuasive enough to come away with half a litre. He then found a workable combination of local trains that took him into Manchester, where he went to the offices of the *Morning Herald*. Here he had to do a great deal of waiting, for which his silent patience stood him in good stead. What he had to ask was found at first less than credible, then contrary to the policies of the paper—and then beyond the permitted decision of their Northern Editor. There was a telephone call to London, but the Editor-in-Chief had already left by air to preside over tonight's test of witchcraft. Mosley came away with no decision reached but sympathetic consideration promised. He got back to Upper Marldale only just in time to dead-heat with the AC(T)'s arrival at his briefing lectern.

"Our main trouble is going to be with crowds, but I propose to use the problem to provide its own solution. Thanks to the publicity given by the media, people are going to flock to Marldale, and it would be disastrous to deny access to the Queen's Highways in a free democracy."

"Even in the interests of public safety?" someone asked.

"The interests of public safety would not be helped by a wave of anti-police animus. On the other hand, there is bound to be some pretty bad driving. The approach roads to Marldale, even along their better stretches, are appalling, and one of my senior colleagues from Traffic has undertaken that they will all be blocked by natural contingencies before dusk: wheels over the edge, a contra-flow of heavy-goods vehicles, an articulated jack-knifed across a narrow bridge. It will be chaos. The public will not be able to complain that they do not have access—but few will get through."

Mosley and Beamish then went, as scheduled, to Priscilla Bladon's house to bring the three witches down to the churchyard. This was done in a Black Maria under armed escort and their cloaks swirled behind them as they were rushed towards the bell tent. There was no doubting from the imperious billowing of her folds that Priscilla Bladon was queen-pin. Susan Bexwell wore her costume with an over-neatness that tended to spoil the illusion. And Deirdre Harrison was unable to wear even fancy dress as if she had any interest in clothes.

The tent had been pitched so that its entrance-flaps

were on the side from which no one but ambushing po-
licemen could see them. A length of dark-painted wattle-
fencing had been erected for the witches to dodge behind.
Lights went on in the tent. The whining of the synthesizers
started. The fabricated silhouettes began their macabre dance
on the canvas sides. Orders were that Mosley was not to
move the women until darkness had had another twenty
minutes to complete its hold. He slipped away to the command post to see the state of the operational log.

The trouble with the Assistant Commissioner (Terrorism) was not that he was steeped in military command. He
was a military commander *manqué*—had never risen above
staff captain. His planning was thorough, his imagination
was lively—up to a point and his efficiency was striking—
but only as far as concerned what he had foreseen.

His radio-reported tracking of the three from the motel
was a model of its kind. He knew that they had settled their
accounts after breakfast this morning, that they had then
split up about Bradcaster in occupations that made them
look very like office-equipment salespersons. The man calling himself Bates and the woman called Sarah Saunders had
lunched together. Halfway through the afternoon, the third
member of the party, obviously their getaway man, picked
up an unobtrusive but souped-up Cortina that he had had
garaged on the edge of town, and drove up towards one of
the outer and upper flanks of Marldale—where he was to
fall foul of one of Traffic's most impenetrable snarl-ups.
Bates and the woman parked in the disused loop of road
that harboured Smoky Joe's. They then went on on foot,
the man carrying a sports bag that might possibly contain
the parts of a readily assembled firearm. The woman had
a black miniature poodle in her arms and was carrying a
small transistor-set to which she was hooked up by an ear-
piece. It seemed that they were going to approach Upper
Marldale by Herbert Garside's—which, as far as Ordnance
Survey knew, was still a charming footpath open to the
public. The AC(T) sent a message up the Nab that laudable
though he had found the interception of Peter Muller, the
couple were to be let through unimpeded.

Mosley returned to the bell tent and told Beamish and

the women to accompany him in close Indian file through the trees, Beamish in the rear as party whip. They had not gone far before Beamish made his way to the front of the column.

"This is not the way back to Miss Bladon's house."

"We're not going to Miss Bladon's house."

"But orders are—"

"Too inflexible," Mosley said. "That's my only criticism of the Assistant Commissioner."

"Really, Mosley—I've backed you up in some dubious situations before now, but on an operation of this magnitude—"

"An operation of this magnitude will come to nothing unless someone has a loop-line for alternative events."

"Really, Mosley, I don't think I can stay with you on this."

"You won't be with me much longer, Sergeant Beamish."

"What do you mean by that?"

"Just think of me as Mr. Flexibility," Mosley said.

He led them up to the Old Tollhouse, whose grounds were one of the most heavily guarded areas. But its guards were a contingent from the Pringle sub-division, all of whom knew Mosley too well to question any on-the-spot order that he gave.

"I want to get these people indoors as quickly and quietly as possible."

And two men came out of the shadows, one of them carrying heavy professional photographic equipment.

"Mr. Mosley? *Morning Herald*. We've been told to meet you here."

"I thought they'd see sense. Come in, gentlemen. This is your one big journalist-of-the-year chance."

He took the party, not into the Tollhouse living-quarters, but into the studio-annexe.

"We are going to secrete ourselves in here. I'm afraid it's going to be a weird vigil, because very shortly I'm going to insist on our sitting in darkness. Sergeant Beamish— now is the time for you to leave."

"I think, perhaps, after all—"

"Leave, Sergeant Beamish!"

"No, Mr. Mosley—I'm in this with you."

"I have another job for you. Why do you think I asked you to find out from Major Hindle how he used to get up here from the village without being seen by any of the gossips? A footpath from the back corner of the garden. I want you to follow that path down. Come outside, and I'll fill you in."

Deirdre had taken off her witch's hat and balanced it on one of the struts of an easel. She was sitting awkwardly on the folds of her cloak.

Mosley went out with Beamish, having first taken from the bag he was carrying a bottle of half-litre size. He was gone some time, and while he was away the women talked desultorily and with only artificial interest in any subject that was brought up.

"News time," Priscilla Bladon said unexpectedly. "I wonder if Bea Cater's radio is still here? Let's see what they're saying about us."

She went into the living-room and came back with a portable set tuned in to Radio Bradcaster. When Mosley returned, they were still agog with a news item. On one of the link roads outside Bradburn someone had driven a car at reckless speed into a telegraph-pole. It was difficult to see how such an accident could have happened on an otherwise deserted highway, unless the steering had gone completely out of control. The vehicle was a twisted write-off, the telegraph-pole had emerged through the boot and the driver was unrecognizable.

They were silent to let Mosley hear the repetition of the headlines at the end of the bulletin. There was a stop-press announcement that the car had been identified from its number-plate as belonging to a senior County Council official. His name was not announced, since the vehicle might well have been stolen, and since the next-of-kin had not yet been informed.

So Tod Hunter had gone to his death in the hope that his family would have the advantage of a newly accepted additional life policy?

"I didn't foresee this," Mosley said. "No one could have

done. Sarah Saunders was carrying a radio, listening to pop music, I expect. If she's heard that news, they'll call the murder off. Dead men's executors don't settle this kind of contract. The Assistant Commissioner's waiting for them to come in through his cordon. He won't even know they're already on their way out—having no doubt dumped their weapons. So even if they are picked up, there'll be nothing to identify them with felonious intent: just another pair of sight-seers. However—"

He went out and conferred with the Pringle men on gate and perimeter duty, making sure they put themselves out of sight. Then he went back indoors and asked for lights out, silence, and no movement—whatever he himself might do.

The patrol lying low along Herbert Garside's footpath were faithful to the AC's orders. They let Reginald Bates and Sarah Saunders pass, even though the pair came so close that they could hear the faint, tinny sound escaping from the ear-piece of their transistor. A few yards further on, the couple stopped.

"Finished!" the woman whispered. "This is it, Reg."

"Why?"

"Hunter's topped himself."

"What now, then? Back the way we came?"

"Like hell. I've had enough of this assault course. And I'm up to my knees in shit and dirt. We'll go on down into the village, just be two more in the crowd, get up to where Des is parked as best we can. And get rid of that bloody gun."

Bates threw the sports bag away from him. A constable retrieved it after they had passed out of hearing.

"My God, Sarge—look what we've got here!"

Bates and Saunders emerged into the heart of the village, strolling, looking about them as if they had never been here before—and as if they were not impressed by what they saw. There were a lot of people out of doors, but they were mostly villagers. Very few had walked down from where they had left their vehicles in the tangle that it was going to take hours to sort out. The shadow dance was still going on inside the tent. The electronic music seemed to be playing the background score from a Hammer film. The pair watched for a few minutes, moving gradually from the churchyard wall to the Square, then quickening their pace up the hill towards the Tollhouse.

It was here that the poodle took a sudden flying leap out of her mistress's arms, furrowed into the overgrown grass of the verge, disappeared into the hedge bottom and was heard to struggle out again higher up. The woman dived after her.

"Oh, for Christ's sake leave her!" the man said. "Haven't we had trouble enough with that damned animal?"

But Sarah Saunders continued to chase the bitch up the hill, across the road, into another ditch, then out again, and so in at the gate of the Old Tollhouse. There was no sign of human activity anywhere along its boundaries.

"Oh, God—not here again!"

But she pursued her pet into the house, through the living-room, into the bedroom where Beatrice Cater's vertebrae had parted at the neck.

"Oh, no! Not here! Come out of it! There's nobody there. They've cleaned it all up."

Then something brushed against her legs. A cat. Boudicca—released by Mosley from the adjacent studio.

"Not you too! Reg—that bloody cat's still here! Remember, you couldn't perform with it watching you? Well old friend, I slung you out once, I'll sling you out again."

And she picked up the cat and flung her out through the open front door. At which all was light, men from the Pringle sub-division seemed to be everywhere, and Mosley was prominent.

"Been here before, have you? Slung a cat out, did you? Couldn't rise to the occasion with her watching, could he? Better take her down to the Assistant Commissioner, Sergeant. Her boy-friend too. Say that if they have any difficulty about what sort of statements we want from them, I'll be down presently to make a few suggestions."

But conversation then stopped, even among the uniformed men who had surrounded Bates and Saunders and were fiddling with handcuffs. Something struck across the moist night air: the church clock of Upper Marldale.

"Good old Beamish!" Deirdre said.

"Bugger me! That's going to cost my management a tidy penny," said the staff photographer.

"Well, I put it to your boss," Mosley told him. "Smuggle my sergeant into that church tower, and your reporters can stay with Crafty Jack for the rest of the evening. Besides, as I pointed out: if he'd exposed our witches as frauds, his circulation would have been back to normal the next morning. But a gift of a playing-field to an impoverished community—that ought to gain him at least a dozen new readers up here in Marldale."

"Have you finished with me?" Deirdre asked. "I don't know whether your sergeant still fancies me—or whether he ever really did. But I think I owe it to myself to go down and find out."

ABOUT THE AUTHOR

"JOHN GREENWOOD" is the pseudonym of a well-known British crime writer who, to the great sorrow of his many followers, recently passed away at his Norwich home. Fortunately for the admirers of the engaging Inspector, Mr. Greenwood has left a legacy in the form of two completed but as-yet-unpublished Mosley novels, which will appear in the near future.

Kinsey Millhone is . . .

"The best new private eye." —The Detroit News

"A tough-cookie with a soft center." —Newsweek

"A stand-out specimen of the new female operatives."
—Philadelphia Inquirer

Sue Grafton is . . .

The Shamus and Anthony Award winning creator of Kinsey Millhone and quite simply one of the hottest new mystery writers around.

Bantam is . . .

The proud publisher of Sue Grafton's Kinsey Millhone mysteries:

- ☐ 26563 "A" IS FOR ALIBI $3.50
- ☐ 26061 "B" IS FOR BURGLAR $3.50
- ☐ 26468 "C" IS FOR CORPSE $3.50